OUR PRINCESS

Mafia Reverse Harem

Leandra Camilli

CONTENTS

CLAIMING HER AGE GAP

CHAPTER 1

Seated on the couch, I had little idea about what I should be doing right now. I took sips from the wine I was holding in my hands and tried to look confident, even though doing so was like moving a mountain. It was so difficult to look confident when I was among several people so different from me.

They were all magnates, richer than I could ever imagine. My father was one of them, but he never gave me more money than he thought I was due.

Not that I had a problem with that, just that it took away some of the freedom that I was supposed to have now that I was 21 years old.

21 years old and still a virgin, I lamented, trying not to think too hard about that. It was a topic that truly made me question the direction that my life took. I didn't want to think too hard about it, knowing that I would just start to question everything I did. If that happened, I was pretty sure that everything would get much worse.

I wore a flimsy, dark red dress that clung to my body, highlighting my curves. It felt a bit too tight, but it wasn't the tighter piece that I had in my wardrobe. I liked tight clothes and I wasn't going to hide that. So much so that I wasn't ashamed of the glances that I caught in my direction. Dirty, older men that should be more concerned about what their wives were doing given that they weren't at home now.

I was so much younger than them that I felt displaced, knowing that the hours were going to keep passing and I wasn't going to be able to talk to any of them. I knew that they wanted to talk, but I was also aware that they just wanted to take me to their bedroom, where they could do whatever they wanted to me.

As if to show me that I was wrong about my assumptions, my eyes caught sight of a shadow that I should have overlooked.

And it wasn't even just a normal, mundane shadow, but a man unlike the rest in the room. The moment my eyes were on him, I knew he was different and younger than everyone else in the room, but also much older than me.

He held a wine glass in his hand as well, but something about the way he was doing that told me that he had a level of self-esteem unmatched. He knew his place in the world, where he stood among all the men in the room, and that he had come here for someone specific.

Thinking back to what my father had said, I knew that that person was none other than me. To save our family, he sold me for his business. I was supposed to marry a Mafia boss, which was ridiculous.

Who in their right mind would agree to something like that? I didn't know, but I had to take the dive anyway. There had been no other choice.

It was my chance to get out from under my father's scrutiny, which was something I had been wanting since I turned 15.

My father was always worried about me, concerned that I was doing something wrong, always keeping me on a tight leash. I found it difficult just to breathe. And the worst thing was that I couldn't even go and see my friends, other than when I had classes.

I had no idea, nevertheless, if that sexy and hot man on the other side of the room was even interested in me. I had no idea if he truly was one of the Mafia bosses that came here just for me. It could be very well that he was here for someone else that didn't have anything to do with me.

I sighed, taking another sip of the wine, noticing that now it was too hot. I didn't even like wines that much. I was only drinking the red wine in the wine glass because I wanted to look the part, even though now I knew that doing so was impossible.

I was pretty much the only woman at the party, after all. All I could see were men and other men, chatting among themselves as if they owned the world.

The man that was on the other side of the room was nothing short of perfect, probably standing over six foot five tall, his dark suit doing very little in terms of hiding his muscles.

They flexed and strained against the material, making me wonder what he looked like without it on. I didn't know anything about the guy yet, but I'd definitely let him take my V-card, if he wanted it.

I could close my eyes and imagine him on top of me, peppering me with passionate kisses that would send me through the roof. I imagined his hot body grinding against mine, making me feel small and insignificant. Was that such an impossible thing to ask for? I didn't think so, which was why, in case he was my promised one, I wondered if I had a good chance of making that happen.

I put the glass with wine back down on the table by my side, saying to myself that I didn't want it anymore. But the real reason why I did that was that I was paralyzed. The man who I thought would never have eyes for me just glanced in my direction and held my gaze.

He was staring at me as if he knew I was his promised one. I couldn't even blink, knowing that he was a man assured of himself who was used to getting everything his way.

But then, he glanced in the other direction, making me wonder when and if I would be able to see his emerald green eyes again.

They were so determined, so resolute, and it was as if he was dissecting me with them when he was looking at me.

But now that his eyes were focused on the old man standing across from him, I felt as if I was finally back to my body, only then to realize that it was nothing more than an illusion, for someone else just caught my attention.

It was another hot guy, too sexy for his own good. He wasn't holding anything in his hands, merely just waltzing in as if he owned the place.

He was blond, with a perfect jawline, and lips that made me want to kiss him right away. It was such a pity that I couldn't, still stuck on this couch as if I was glued to it.

I thought that he was just one of the guests, but then my brain started to make connections and I knew that it couldn't be just a coincidence. My father had said that I was going to be able to choose between three men, and that had to be the second one. He was talking to one of the guests, smiling and showing his perfect teeth.

Even though I was so far away from him that I felt he was unreachable, I could tell that he was pretty tall. Probably a head taller than me, and that was me being conservative with my estimate. I could just imagine myself melting in his arms, his body dominating me in ways I never thought possible.

I was just so horny, so ashamed of still being a virgin. It wasn't that I was so because I was to blame, but that my father always scared off possible partners.

He wanted to keep me pure and innocent, even though that didn't work. It only worked in the sense that I had never even kissed, but my mind was still as dirty as any other's.

I glanced to the left, deciding that I shouldn't keep looking at that guy. Chances were, he was going to turn his head to the right and find me on the couch, paralyzing me just like that other guy did. If that happened, I would certainly do something stupid.

He would notice that I was sweating even though the room was cold and that the AC was turned on. I couldn't let that happen. I couldn't make a fool of myself and I wasn't going to.

The only problem with that was that my eyes just caught sight of another hot man entering the room, his coconut hair flying in the gentle wind.

That's it. Those were the three guys that my father said were my options, and they were at the party. They came here searching for me and were going to find me, unless I made a run for it.

Before he could turn his eyes where I was and find me, I stood up and walked out of there as fast as my legs could take me.

When I was crossing the doorway to the kitchen and then to

the outside of the house, I already felt a lot more confident and better.

It didn't matter what happened now, I wasn't going to walk back into the house.

CHAPTER 2

When I was outside, I could finally breathe. A comfy chair was positioned by the pool, where I sat and crossed my legs. It was as if I was trying to protect the part of me that I wanted to lose, even though that didn't make any sense.

I had my phone with me, which was pretty much the only thing keeping me company right now. The minutes ticked by, nothing happened, and I figured that I was finally out of sight and safe.

If those guys had indeed come here seeking me, they weren't going to find me here. They were probably too busy with their friends and the other guests, chatting and cracking jokes among themselves.

They were having fun, which was something I wasn't.

I sighed, closing my eyes tightly and thinking back to all the men that I spotted at the party. They were so hot, making me wonder if I shouldn't just give up on my current life and go away with one of them. I was pretty sure that at least one of them would accept that.

I reopened my eyes when I found out that a pair of footsteps were coming toward the swimming pool. I thought that I was dreaming, but then I realized that I wasn't. One of the guys that I saw before was by the swimming pool, his hands in his pockets.

He was just looking ahead at nowhere in particular, making me wonder what was going on in his mind. He was completely alone, and it didn't seem that he was waiting for someone. Rather, it was as if he was waiting for me to do something.

At least, that's what I was thinking.

He was the first guy I saw before, with pitch-black hair and some beard on his face still to be made. I couldn't help but imagine what I would feel if I were to move my hand around his chin, scratching his beard.

The thought of doing that was enough to make me question what I was even doing right now. I was such a stupid, cowardly fool.

Not only that, but the guy by the swimming pool was probably not even thinking about me, unless he really was one of the ones that composed my choices for husband.

I thought that nothing was going to happen, until he turned his head slightly in my direction, saying, "You can stop looking now. I know you are."

His words caught me off guard, making me jump in the chair where I was seated. I almost fell off of it.

"What?"

"You can stop looking, or you can tell me everything that's going on in your mind. I'm curious. I've always been very curious. You are Elena Marchesi, aren't you?" He asked, turning around slowly and then shuffling over to me.

I should be running away as fast as I could, but I couldn't. I was as frozen in place as I was before, knowing that he was coming for me. I thought that he was going to grab me and yank me off the chair, but then he rounded where I was seated, stopping right behind me.

Then, he crouched, putting his head right next to mine.

The command that he had over me was utterly destructive and he was well aware of it. So much so that he didn't hold back when he murmured, "You are such a thing of beauty.

You are beautiful, perfect as you are, and I'm already obsessed with you. I want to be with you. I want to be your king, but the question is: do you want the same? Do you want to be my Queen?"

That's what he asked, but I knew that he didn't expect an answer right at the moment. If anything, he was biding his time, trying to ease me into thinking that he was the one. It finally crossed my mind that it was happening. It was finally happening.

One of the men that were part of my choices was already hitting on me, trying to convince me that he was the one I should pick.

But I didn't even know the other guys yet. I didn't even know their names and only now was I finding out how hot they were.

And not just hot, but also extremely sexy, so much so that just the guy that was behind me was making my pussy wet. It was soaked. I had never felt so warm and never sweated so much before in my life.

"What are you going to do now? What is your name?" I asked, my voice throaty and dry right now, even though I was drinking wine not too long ago.

"I just want to get to know you better. Elena... I think you should know it. You deserve to know it. My name is Marcello and I came all the way from Italy for you. You were in my dreams. Your father showed me how beautiful you are before I came, and I know you are the one I want. I want to take you to my bed and make you happy. Do you want that too? Do you want to find out how happy I can make you feel?"

When he asked that, he planted his lips onto my neck, making my body shudder and shiver. His lips were so hot, and they stayed connected to my skin for minutes, just feeling it for what it was. Time passed and it was as if he wasn't going to disconnect his lips from my skin anytime soon.

Each second that passed and his lips were still connected to my skin, I felt my breathing quickening. I felt the world around me turning black, my pores pushing out more sweat drops, my hands clenching.

I wanted him to play with my pussy, to rub his finger over it until he made me come, until he made me feel as much pleasure as he was promising me, but I was still inexperienced and afraid of what might happen. And my lack of decision right now was annoying me so much. I felt as if I was failing myself.

He put his hand next to my breast, making me fear that he was going to go under the dress, pinch my nipple, and do whatever else he wanted to do with it. I didn't need to look into his eyes to know what he was thinking right now.

He was taking advantage of me, figuring out that I was a virgin and that I could do nothing to stop him. He was just like that. Marcello was used to having everything his way, including kissing the neck of a woman he didn't even know. I mean, he just met me in person for the first time, knew what my voice sounded like, and was using everything he could to his advantage.

His lips were still pressing against my neck and I was wondering how I was going to deal with the hickey that he was going to leave. It was going to be a pretty noticeable, colorful hickey that even my father, who was going blind, was going to notice. And when he noticed it, he would ask me what happened and I would have no answers for him.

Things were as simple as that in my life, especially when such a hot guy was drooling all over me. I should be feeling pleased that I was so sexy to the point of making him fall for me, but I wasn't behaving that way.

Rather, my body was frozen where I was and incapable of moving even one of my fingers. His hand roaming my breast, he was getting so dangerously close to my nipple that I couldn't hide my moan when it escaped through my lips.

What made me a little less concerned about the consequences of that was knowing that everyone else was at the party, incapable of hearing my moan.

When he noticed that enough was enough, he pulled his head back, smiling devilishly at me. I didn't need to turn my head all the way to see his face completely to know that. The smile on his face was evil and perfect, drawing me even more to him.

I wanted to be all over him, to be in Marcello's arms, but I knew that that wasn't possible.

As he moonwalked away from me, he widened his smile before saying, "I'm going to be here somewhere at the party, and you can come looking for me when you're ready. Remember that you have only one choice and that I'm not willing to share. You are my girl to keep."

CHAPTER 3

I should be angry that Marcello did what he did when I was so vulnerable, but the truth was that I just found it too hot. If anything, I wanted him to come where I was, which was my bedroom.

It was eerily silent at night, stars twinkling behind the window. With the moon rising over the buildings, I knew that it was already time to sleep and that I should take off my dress.

And that I did, kicking away my high heels when I heard a noise coming from the outside. For a moment, I didn't think much of it, but then I realized that it was nearing me. It could be a criminal or an assassin, and I didn't want to risk it.

I was going to shut the window, shout as loudly as I could so that the guards rushed over here in a heartbeat, and then the thug would be locked behind bars, perhaps even spending the rest of his life in jail. Or maybe, if he was unlucky enough, he would find himself with a bullet in his head.

I sped over to the window, grabbing it when I realized that a man was climbing the house, popping up right in front of me with a huge smile on his face. It was the smile of someone who knew that he just won the race that I didn't even know we were competing in until it was too late. He placed his hand under the window, making it impossible for me to shut it. I tried to, but I couldn't.

At the end of the day, I was much smaller and weaker than him, and he was using his strength to his advantage. I noticed that he was the second guy that I found at the party.

He should have already gone out with everyone else, but I

didn't think he cared about that. If anything, it had been his choice to come to my room when everybody else was already out.

Now that I was thinking about it, he was probably not much different from the first guy that came to me when I was by the swimming pool. And that made it all the better.

I was scared, but there was no denying that he came here just for me.

"No need to be scared of me," he joked, jumping into the room as he stood before me. He was so much taller, so much bigger than me that I had no other choice but to scoot away from him. I moonwalked toward one of the walls, realizing that my butt was pressing against it.

He stood before me, approaching me as he planted his hands against the wall. I thought that he was going to kiss me right away, but he was just holding me with his gaze.

It was making me feel uncomfortable and as if he was planning on doing unspeakable things to me. Just imagining them, my pussy was throbbing and wet, wondering what it would be like if I lost my virginity to him.

"I'm going to call the guards and then you will go to jail," I threatened, soon realizing that my warning didn't mean anything to him. If anything, it amused him. He was looking at me with a dirty smile on his face. It infuriated me that he was so full of himself, just like the first guy. He was presuming that I was going to fall in love with him instead of the first one.

"You're not going to do any of that, Elena. I know that you've been thinking about me this whole time. When you saw me at the party, you knew I was the one. There's no point in denying that."

As soon as he expressed that, he took one hand off the wall and settled it on my shoulder. I shivered, feeling how warm his skin was. I felt so exposed, knowing that I was almost naked in front of this huge man.

I had no idea he was so audacious – to the point of barging into my room without warning. He was so full of himself and instead of hating that, I found it hot.

"I haven't been thinking about you. I could never. I didn't even know you were at the party," I argued, realizing that he found that funny. The smirk on his face told me as much.

He moved his hand around my shoulder, down my arm, stopping it when he grabbed my hand. It was big. I wasn't going to deny that. His hand was massive, heavy, and mine was nothing when compared to it.

He asserted his dominance and I could do nothing about it.

Realizing that I was under his spell, he settled his hand on my waist and then took me to the bed, laying me on it. A moment later, he was on top of me, his fingers moving until they were under my bra. He lowered it, exposing my breast. It was as if time was moving in slow motion for me, which in turn was quickening my breathing. I had never felt so hot, so desperate to be with a man.

I could feel his acid breath against my face, his lips dreadfully close to touching mine. He didn't, instead gliding his head down so that he was where my breast was. He parted his lips, then wrapped them around my nipple.

As soon as they were touching my nipple, applying pressure on it, I felt as if I was going to explode. I had never felt so much pleasure before, so much arousal at the same time.

And that was when I knew that he wasn't even doing anything special yet, just swirling his tongue around my nipple, applying pressure when needed. He was in utter control of me, so much so that I urgently tried to grab at his shirt, tearing it. He didn't mind it, just groaning deeper against my nipple.

"You are so delicious," the man murmured, loving the way that I melted under his dominance. The more he wetted my nipple with his lips, the more I wanted him and the more I wanted to know one more thing about the man.

"What is your name?" I croaked, feeling as if it took everything I had to ask that question. The first few seconds, he didn't behave as if he was going to answer me, but then he thrust his head back, holding my gaze.

"It's Amadeo and I want you to choose me. You have to. I'm the promised one. I'm the man you want to be with..." Amadeo murmured, opening another smile as he showed me how overconfident he was.

"You are such a jerk," I replied, knowing that what I just said didn't mean anything to him. Amadeo was just that kind of man. He was always full of himself, overconfident, and a womanizer.

Then, with a sudden thrust of his arm, he ripped off my bra, chucking it over his head. I didn't have any time to react, loathing the fact that I was going to have to ask my father for another one. I didn't have that many bras in my collection, I swore.

"Look at you. Look at how exquisite you are. You are just perfect, made for me. The more you try to deny that, the more you assure me that that's the case."

He lowered his head again, encircling his lips around my nipple one more time. But this time, it was different. He was taking care of my other nipple, loving it the way he knew how.

What he was doing to them, twirling his tongue around them, was enough to take me through the roof and beyond it. My body started to shake, my eyes closed, and I reached my orgasm.

It was different from anything I thought it was going to be like, especially when it came to what he was doing. He merely pleased my nipples and I already hit my climax.

That was just my inexperience speaking louder than everything I knew about sex. If I were more experienced, that certainly wouldn't have happened.

When my body stopped shaking, I reopened my eyes and found that Amadeo was still on top of me, breathing leisurely.

I thought that we were going to go on, but then his phone started to buzz in the pocket of his pants and, when he grabbed it, it took no more than a glance at the screen for him to hop off the bed.

I sat up on the bed speedily, my mouth gaping. I had no idea what just happened, just that the man that was bringing me so much pleasure wasn't on top of me anymore. He beelined to the window, jumping through it after saying, "Remember what I said and what I did tonight. There's still more after what we did."

My mouth was still gaping. Just like that, Amadeo left the

room as my body went cold. I thought we were going to fuck. I assumed he was going to be the one to take my virginity, which was something that still deeply ashamed me.

And then I dropped my back on the bed, feeling frustrated. Was I even going to get to meet the third guy before the promised date?

CHAPTER 4

I walked outside the house, thinking that I wasn't going to see anything special other than the swimming pool. The water was pristine, sparkling under the hot sunlight.

With just my bikini on, I knew I looked stunning, which was one of the reasons why I had a tight-lipped smile on my face. When I walked by some of the guards in the hallway behind me, the glances that they gave me reconfirmed that.

I was a curvy, hourglass-shaped girl and I didn't feel any shame regarding that. I was beautiful, just like Amadeo had expressed before he disappeared.

Around the swimming pool, I couldn't perceive anything other than trees and several more trees. They hid the wall behind it, and the latter was tall and thick enough to make most criminals and journalists think at least thrice before trying to break in. I felt safe here, which was something that most residents in the city couldn't say about where they lived.

I closed my eyes, appreciating the sunlight when I realized that I wasn't alone. I thought I was going to be, but I couldn't ignore the man that was lying on the lounge chair. With his head propped on his arms, without his shirt, and with a pair of shorts covering his thighs, he was hot and sexy, making me stop right in my tracks.

I didn't suspect I was going to find one of the other 'interested parties' still at the property. I thought that they had all already left. It was one of the reasons why I had left my guard down today, after all.

He didn't shoot up and lurch toward me when I stopped walking. I presumed he was going to do that, but he didn't even move.

Rather, he just continued lying down on the lounge chair, his dark sunglasses hiding his eyes from me. I had no idea if he was looking at me and I wasn't going to find that out, unless I neared him.

Just like the time I was in my room, I felt exposed. The bikini did little in terms of shielding my body against his presence, and it was spicy enough to force me to step towards him. Having no other choice, I did just so.

When I was a couple of feet across from him, I asked, "What are you doing in my backyard?"

For the first few seconds, the man didn't say anything, opting to stay silent. His body was flawless, I noticed, dissecting it with my eyes. The curves that defined his chest, his abs, his torso, and his shoulders – they were drool-inducing.

I wanted to reach out and delineate his curves with my hands, but I couldn't. I was far too inexperienced and I knew that it was a trap. The moment I did something like that, the first thing he would do would be to shoot up from the lounge chair, sweep me up in his arms, and do whatever else he harbored in his mind.

The crooked smile on his face didn't lie that he was aware that I was here.

When I was going to add to what I asked before, he responded to my question, "I'm not like the other guys. I'm not going to go after you. You have to come after me."

I couldn't even wrap my head around what he just said, shoving my hands against my waist as I felt that his words were absurd. He assumed that I was going to be the one obsessed over him and not the other way around? If so, he was out of his mind.

When I opened my mouth to express that, he shot up from the lounge chair, lunging at me and falling with me into the swimming pool. I felt my body being immersed in the water, struggling to stay afloat.

I didn't know how to swim, my arms and legs moving uncontrollably. I thought I was going to drown, but then I felt that he was around me. His arms held me securely and I could feel his firm muscles against the skin of my body, holding me where I was.

He was swinging his legs shyly to keep both of us afloat, my head just over the water. His face was right in front of me and I could finally see his eyes, his dark sunglasses nowhere to be seen. His minty breath snuck out of his mouth, and it was intoxicating and was making me want to kiss him, even though I knew I shouldn't.

I knew what his plan was. He caught me off guard when I was least expecting him to, and now was using this moment to capture my heart. I wasn't going to allow him to, though. I was stronger than that and far more determined than he thought I was.

His hand slithered down, finding the lower part of my bikini. His eyes locked with mine and I wondered what he was thinking. His hands were inches away from finding my pussy, and I just remembered that I hadn't shaved. Why would I have done that when I didn't think I was going to have sex anytime soon?

His finger toyed with my skin, showing me just how close he was to touching my pussy, even through the cloth of the bikini. The tentative smile on his face showed me that he wasn't even close to thinking about stopping.

"I'm Aldo, by the way, and I'm going to show you now why you should choose me."

"Is that so? I thought you were going to say that you had come here just for yourself and that you have no expectations. After all, you said that I was going to be the one going after you."

"Smart girl," he murmured, putting his lips very close to the curve of my neck, breathing against it as he made me feel shivers running down my spine. Gosh, whatever he was thinking he was doing, it was working. I was dissolving in his arms, bathing in his strength and how much smaller he made me feel when compared to the proportions of his body.

Studying his face, I could tell that he was much older than me. The wrinkles around his eyes, the texture of his skin, the confidence in his pupils told me as much.

Despite the age gap, which I was assuming was around 10 years, I didn't feel more intimidated than I already was. In fact, it was telling me to do the one thing that I was pretty sure was in his mind, too.

Realizing that, I nodded, giving him the go-ahead. With the go-ahead, he snuck his finger under the lower part of my bikini, grazing my pussy with it. When his finger was pressing against it, against my pussy folds, I arched my back, letting a moan out. If anyone was close by, and I was certain someone was, then they just heard it.

His finger sliding up and down over my pussy deliciously slowly, he had me where he wanted. I never suspected that he was going to be right when he said what he did before, that I was going to go after him. He wasn't even doing much. He was just browsing my pussy with his finger, rubbing over it in small and controlled movements, and it was perfect.

Aldo hit all the right spots, liquifying me so much I thought I was going to become one with the water. As if to torment me more than he already was, he crept another finger under my bikini, pressing it against my sensitive skin.

As he performed controlled movements with it, I thought I was going to come and, for sure, it seemed that I was. Then, Aldo added another finger under my bikini, drawing more small circles with it and his two other fingers over my sensitive skin. It was liberating, intoxicating, and my breathing was quickening. In no time at all, I shut my eyes tightly when I felt that it was too late. I was trying to hold my orgasm back, but it was pointless. It rushed out, making my body shake and grind against his firm muscles.

When it was over, he was still holding me tightly in his arms. I suspected that, as long as he held me in them, nothing could harm me.

The seconds ticked by and when I realized that our little fun was over, I ordered, "Take me out of the water."

He widened his smirk, saying, "Whatever you wish, princess."

CHAPTER 5

Everything that happened that day was going to forever be ingrained in my mind. I thought I was going to find the guys at the estate the day after that one, but I didn't.

And I scoured the whole place for them, but I didn't find them. I had no idea what happened to Marcello, Amadeo, and Aldo, but everything that occurred between us was still fresh in my mind and I wanted to repeat it all.

The only problem was that no other man could satisfy me the way they did.

I was by the window of my room, looking outside and checking out the backyard. Sighing, I was so frustrated with my life.

All of those guys did whatever they wanted to me and then left me with nothing. They didn't even take my virginity, which ground my gears.

As if to say that I was wrong about that, I found a piece of paper shyly flying into the room. I reached out with my hand, snatching it midair. What was going on here? I asked myself, turning the paper in my hand so that I could read it.

As my eyes moved from left to right and vice versa, I felt as though I was discovering a new country. I thought that those jerks had already forgotten about me, but that didn't appear to be the case. In the letter, they said that they were going to come to do their manly duty and that I should be patient.

How much time were we talking about? I didn't know, but the part about being patient wasn't going to work.

Just as I was turning around, the door to my room started to open. I took a step backward, trying to understand how this was happening. The door should be closed.

After all, I locked it with the key. But it was as if everything was playing with my mind right now, for the person that was walking into the room wasn't just one guy, but rather all three men from before.

They had dirty smiles on their faces, as if they knew they had me under their full control, which was pretty much the case. I was paralyzed, thinking that this might be the moment I had been looking for. They were going to take my V-card and I wasn't going to be able to do anything about it. To be honest, I welcomed it.

"Sorry for keeping you waiting," Marcello teased, marching toward me as he pushed me against the wall, peppering my neck with several kisses. Aldo was right behind him, ripping off my pajamas and roaming his hand over the side of my body. It was calloused, rough, and he knew how to apply pressure when needed with his fingers.

Amadeo took me from there, tossing me over on the bed. I looked up, noticing that all the three guys now surrounded me. Then, in a matter of seconds, they started to take off their clothes. Everything happened in slow motion for me. I could finally see the perfection of their bodies, the curves that their muscles followed, and how easily they flexed.

Licking my lips, I wagged my finger to make them move toward me. The fact that the door was still open didn't bother me. If anybody was watching this, they were welcomed to join in.

Aldo launched himself toward me, landing heavily on the bed. He yanked me toward him, his fingers digging into my skin.

But even though he was being quite hard on me, I could still feel that he was being careful. I moaned, loving the way his fingers grazed my skin and how fast he was bringing me closer to my orgasm, even though I knew that this time it wasn't going to be as easy to reach it.

It was as if time had frozen around me, I could feel that something flashed in his eyes. Maybe it was the fact that he didn't want to share me with his friends. It was difficult for him to do that when they were also extremely sexy and hot, making me want to be with all of them at the same time.

His finger slithered to where my pussy was, his movement controlled and tremendously slow. I couldn't help but wonder what was going on in his mind, but I didn't have to wonder about that for long. I knew that he was going to claim his prize right now.

Without his pants and underwear, I could finally see what his cock was like. Being almost 10 inches in length, it was more massive than anything I had seen on Pornhub, and I knew that that was putting it mildly. I couldn't help but wonder how much pain I was going to feel when he was inside of me, and I had a hint that it was going to be a lot.

His hands gliding up and down my thighs, I knew I couldn't wait much longer. Supposing that, the next thing I did was to shoot my hand where his dick was, grabbing it. When I seized it, I felt like it was going to explode in my grasp right away, but it didn't.

With everything around me as if it was frozen, I started to move my hand up and down along his cock. Up and down it went, rewarding him with immense pleasure. So much so that it was easy to read what was in his mind. He wanted to be pounding in and out of me and he wasn't going to wait much longer until he could make that happen.

As I jacked him off, I felt a firm and determined hand taking me to the other side of the bed. It took me no more than a second to realize that it was Marcello. He wasn't happy watching his buddy doing everything he wanted to me and wanted a piece of me as well.

It was the first time in my life that so many men showed interest in me, to the point of fighting between themselves for me.

His hands shot to my breasts, fumbling with them and making short work of me. Even if I was trying not to feel turned on, it wouldn't have worked. His hands were as callous as his friends', but also bigger, needier, and he knew where all of my weak spots were, even though this was only the second time he was doing this to me.

"You have no idea how long I've been waiting for this," he murmured into my ear, nibbling on my earlobe.

I didn't have much time to think about what he just said, softening my whole body when his fingers started to tweeze my nipples. They were big and engorged, red and hard. Each time his fingers pressed and applied pressure on them, it was like I was on the moon.

I moaned, arching my back one more time when I realized that Amadeo was between my legs. I didn't have much time to process what was going on, knowing that he was going to make me feel so loved it was going to be impossible not to pick him.

He thrust his tongue out, flicking it up and down over my flower. Each lick sent shockwaves of pleasure through my whole body, making me rock, convulse, and feel that I was forever going to be theirs. Not to mention that it was going to be difficult to choose who took my virginity when the time was right for that.

The bed sheets were covered in sweat, soaked in it. My hands desperately tried to grab and hold on to them, but it was a lost cause. While Amadeo was still lapping up and worshiping my pussy's folds, Marcello laid me down on the floor, moving so that he was on top of me.

I couldn't waste another second, launching my legs around his body. My cunt pressing up against his crotch, I begged him to come inside of me. I wanted him to breach me, to breed me, to do whatever else he wanted to do to me, and that behavior of mine was everything he needed.

He moved down, licking my nipple over and over with his needy tongue, each lick making me feel as if he was shooting me through the roof and beyond it. I curved my back, curled my toes, and felt my snatch getting soaped and wet with my juices, knowing that this wasn't even the beginning of our love.

Things were going to jump to the next level in the next few seconds, and I couldn't wait for that.

CHAPTER 6

Grinding my body against him, I turned around so that they all knew what I wanted from them. Marcello, Amadeo, and Aldo remained where they were, analyzing me with their gaze. They were assessing what the situation was truly like, what they should be doing. When they were satisfied with that, one of them produced a blindfold, which he secured around my head. With my eyes now covered and darkened, I felt even more submissive.

I knew what their end game was. They were going to take my virginity, but since they couldn't do that at the same time, they had to do a little trick. Whoever was going to breach me for the first time, I wasn't going to know it. I would never know what the answer to that question was.

I felt fingers moving over my waist, parting my asscheeks. Then, a nose neared my asscrack, breathing it. I didn't stop to think about who was doing that. It was more than obvious that he was the chosen one, the one that was going to impale me with his mighty member for the first time.

I took a deep breath in when I felt his dick nudging my orifice. It was just the beginning of the moment I'd always been waiting for, but it was already everything I thought it was going to be. Then, he just slid it in, going through every barrier and even popping my hymen.

There. It happened and I loved it. I just lost my virginity and it was everything I presumed it was going to be. And holy fuck, he was so deep inside of me I didn't think he could go any deeper.

I could feel his shaft nudging the end of my tunnel, something I thought impossible.

He didn't say anything and, moments later, I felt a hand cracking open my mouth. Whoever it was, I would never know, and I didn't have much time to ponder that. His cock was easing into my mouth and stretching my lips to levels I never thought possible.

Pain flared up in my whole body, but it wasn't anything compared to the level of pleasure that he was rewarding me with. It was invigorating, spreading to every inch of my skin, and I knew that more was going to come.

As if to show me how right I was, the third and last Mafioso swooped under me, gracing my boobs and teats with his needy tongue. One lick after the other, making sure that he graced all the right spots, he overloaded all of my senses, and that was putting it mildly.

The guy behind me started to pound in and out of me, slapping my butt over and over. It wasn't enough that he stole my virginity, but he also needed to claim me now, and little did I know that a lot more was going to come after that.

He wasn't even half done with me. I assumed I was going to have enough time to catch my breath, but then, when I thought that he was going to start creaming inside of me, he pulled out. For a moment, I didn't know what was going on in his mind, but then his plan cleared up for me.

The guy under me then swooped away, putting himself behind me and replacing his buddy. Not wasting any time, he pushed his shaft all the way in, until he was also breaching through every barrier possible that I had put up for him, even though I didn't mean to. It was just something that happened and that I had no control over. My body was like that.

The guy behind me continued to pound in and out of me, pain and pleasure flaring up all over my body, making me feel that I was going to pass out. And surely, that would have happened if it weren't for the fact that I was already orgasming one more time.

"You are ours. You are ours and ours alone. I thought we weren't going to share you, but that was never the case. It's better to share you because we know that we can't and that we shouldn't compete between ourselves."

My mind was in such disarray that I couldn't even make out who said that. It was too late for that anyway, my body rocking over and over, losing control of all my senses.

The guy that was ramming in and out of me continued to do so for what felt like hours, and my mouth was so filled up with the dick that was inside of it that I couldn't even say anything.

Then, as if to make my torment even worse than it already was, the guy that was ravaging my mouth decided to take things up a notch. He grabbed my hair and started to shove my head up and down, deep-throating me in a way I never thought feasible.

I really thought that they had semblances of mercy for me, but now I realized that that was nothing more than wishful thinking. They craved being inside of me, they wanted to turn me into their doll, and I could do nothing more than obey them.

Moments later, my body started to shake and rock as I reached another climax. I heard a sneer, one of the guys showing me that he didn't feel anything other than absolute pride in the way he was manhandling me now.

Seconds after that, the moment I'd been waiting for all this time took place. The man that was eating my pussy raw finally started to throb inside of me, shooting his come in there.

Just as I'd presumed, it was going to be nigh impossible to choose just one of them to be my forever husband. I was going to have to think about that clearly, giving it enough thought so that my mind was fully focused on the right answer.

He pulled out of me, patting my shoulder as he made me think that he wasn't going to continue what they were all doing. But then, as if to show me how wrong I was, he was soon replaced by his last buddy. I had no idea who he was, but given how hungry he was, I was certain that he was going to do me a lot harder than the guy before, even though that was almost impossible to accomplish.

His fingers grabbed my waist, tugging me hardly toward him. I didn't have enough time, his cock nudging my orifice before it was too late. Moments later, he was inside of me all the way and I just realized that he was the same guy that was ravaging my mouth before.

My mouth hung open, my lips loose, and I knew that things were far from over. I heard a pair of footsteps beelining to me, one of the Mafia men from before standing right in front of me. When he was there, he grabbed my hair just like his buddy did, shoving my head down. I had just about enough time to open my mouth wide so that he didn't hurt me too much.

When my mouth was filled up with his dick, I started to swirl my tongue around it, but doing so was fruitless and pointless. His dick was far too thick, far too big, and far too veiny for something like that to make him feel any more pleasure than he already was.

But it was enough that I was pleasing him, showing me just how important he was to me. I could feel his balls slapping against my chin, and it was such a pity that I couldn't use my hands to play with them.

I was pretty sure that they were laden with his milk, and I couldn't help but wonder what it was going to be like when he was creaming inside my mouth, too.

Concluding that, I was certain that he was thinking the same thing. He had to be. He had been dreaming about this moment this whole time. In the meantime, I hoped that when they were all creaming inside my pussy, that I was going to give them triplets. One for each of them. It was going to be magical, something I never thought reachable.

"God, you're so fucking hungry. You are insatiable. You are perfect," I heard one of the mafiosos murmuring behind my ear, kissing my neck after he was done with that. As he traced the curve of my neck with his lips and tongue, I couldn't help but urge the last guy to do what was his duty. I wanted him to breach my asshole as well, to take my other virginity.

This wasn't going to feel complete unless I also lost my ass' virginity.

Then, as if to show me how important I was to them, they stopped everything they were doing. They moved away from me, leaving me gasping for air on the floor.

I just remembered that the door was still open, which meant that some of the guards and house workers were probably watching this. I couldn't help but feel a little amused at how flabbergasted they probably were.

I didn't want to be thinking about that for much longer, turning around on the floor so that they knew what I craved.

CHAPTER 7

I reopened my eyes, remembering that I still had the blindfold covering them. I tried to take it off, but then I remembered that I shouldn't do that. I couldn't do that because I didn't want to piss them off. I knew what would happen if I did that.

"Breed me," I muttered, earning a sneer from one of the mafiosos. He tore the blindfold off, showing me that he was none other than Marcello.

I didn't know if he was the one that first took my virginity, but the smile on his face was telling me that he possibly was. His dick dangled in front of his ball sack, making me lick my lips. It was nothing short of massive, gleaming under the sunlight.

It was covered in my pussy juices, showing me that he had been in there for a pretty long time. Time enough to make him miss feeling my walls clenched around his manhood, too. I noticed that he'd shaved too, showing me that he'd always been prepared for this moment. He knew that he was going to do me tonight.

"You're such a little princess. You are desperate, eager to be fucked, and all you want is a man inside of you. I like girls like you. You are always so perfect."

I didn't say anything to rebuke him, knowing that there was nothing that could be said anyway.

"Just breed me already. Make me yours. Make me eternally yours."

He peeked over his shoulder, sneering with his friends. They knew what they should do, Marcello grabbing my legs and throwing them over his shoulders. My flower was right in front of his mouth, and he wasted no time before thrusting his tongue out, licking my folds.

They were already wet, but that was beside the point. He just wanted to worship me further than he already did, showing me just how important I was to him right now.

It wasn't just about showing me that they were sexy and hot, but that they were obsessed with me. They craved being inside of me, to claim every part of me, and they were going to do just that.

Moments later, I felt my body moving, his shaft pressing against my rugged orifice. He was going to impale my asshole and it was going to be the most intoxicating thing that ever happened in my life.

Seconds later, he breached the first barrier, going all the way in. Accommodating him inside of my rectum was even more difficult than it was when he was in my womb, but that was okay.

It was so because I was finally going to be able to tell all of my friends that I lost my virginity in every possible way and that they couldn't poke fun at me anymore.

"Gosh, you're so insatiable," he hissed, rolling his hips as he pounded in and out of me in every way conceivable, showing me just how careful he was being right now. His pace was slow in the beginning, but he soon picked it up, turning me into his little doll.

When my body rocked and convulsed one more time, even breathing was painful. My body was covered in sweat, my fingers trying to grab at his shoulders, finding nothing more than slippery skin.

Moments later, his dick erupted, shooting milk after milk of everything that made him the man he was.

He pushed me away from him, depositing me on the floor. I thought that was going to be it, but then I remembered that the other mafiosos were still here with us.

One of them grabbed me from behind, impaling my orifice with a single thrust. He was all the way inside of me in less than a second, his pace slow in the beginning, as if to exude his care. Nevertheless, I didn't fall for it. If there was one thing that he and his friends couldn't feel, it was mercy.

I didn't even have enough time to catch my breath when he was already erupting inside of me, turning me into his little thing. He thought of me as his plaything, which was exactly what I wanted.

But then, I realized that things were far from over. The last mafioso, whose name was Aldo, still hadn't had his way with my rectum. To make up for that, he snatched me with his rough hands, turned me around quickly, and then shoved his thick and shaft dick all the way in.

When he was balls-deep, he started to roll his hips, and differently from the first two guys that came before him, his pace was frenetic from the get-go. His balls slapping against my ass cheeks, I moaned wildly, feeling as if the world was going to explode.

Then, I convulsed one more time, arching my back and curling my toes. Breathing was painful, but no more than a little nuisance. I reopened my eyes, finding out that Aldo was still right on top of me.

Then, he pulled out, but when I thought that they were just going to move away and out of the room, they decided to surprise me. Surrounding my tiny and trembling body, they started to jack off, creaming all over me seconds later. I could feel their sticky, hot cum all over my skin, painting me in white.

If my skin was already warm before, now it was melting.

I had made my choice. I wasn't going to stay with just one of them. I was going to be with all of the mafiosos and they were all going to be my husbands. There couldn't be another way.

SELLING HER AGE GAP

CHAPTER 1

Being rich didn't mean that I could do anything I wanted. In fact, it was the opposite. When I learned that my father wanted to marry me to a stranger, I was furious. So furious that he ended up putting me on this ship, which was headed toward Europe. He didn't even tell me what country it was. Just that I needed to keep my head low and pretend that nothing was happening.

But that was difficult to do especially when everything that could go wrong was. I had just walked into my room on the ship when I realized that something in it was missing. It was something important to me. It was given to me by my grandmother when she was still alive.

It was a comb. She gave it to me for my 13th birthday and I still remembered it fondly. So much so that I didn't throw it away when it started to break. I kept it with me, always using it when I needed to comb my hair.

I looked around everywhere in the room, but I didn't find the comb.

Was there a suspect? There was and I didn't want to think about it. I didn't want to admit that she was such an asshole that she was doing this to me.

Nevertheless, I jumped out of the room before spinning to the right. Putting one foot forward, I started to march toward her room. I could feel the ship swaying left and right on the ocean. It was making me a little dizzy, but it was nothing that was going to impede me from doing the right thing.

My blood was boiling. I had never felt so angry before in my life.

A few seconds later, I stopped in front of the door to her room. I wasted no time before rapping on it. If she was still in there, then she was going to come out and give me my comb back. There was no other way that this could play out.

I wasn't going to forgive her for this, though.

And just when I thought I heard footsteps coming from the other side of the door, I heard someone coming my way from the left. I turned to see who it was, because I was that curious and also because I had the attention span of a goldfish, when I then bumped against him.

My eyes went up as I realized that it was a huge man that just bumped into me. He was so huge that he made me feel incredibly small, even though I wasn't a small girl. He had something in his hand, which appeared to be a book.

The sweat on his forehead showed me that he was in a hurry. To go where, I didn't know, but I already wanted to find out. He regarded me with a lack of sympathy, as if he couldn't care less about me. I should be angry that that was his reaction, but I felt the opposite. It was the first time that I was in the presence of a man who didn't want to fall to his knees right away, and then there was a flash of something in his eyes which showed me that he thought I was hot.

I felt some heat rising to my cheeks. He was handsome and it flattered me that he thought that way about me. My eyes went down slowly, taking in the curves and the lines of his body. They were perfect, not too harsh, and not too round, either. And even though he wore a suit, I could tell that his body was well-built.

The man was built like a tank was what I was trying to say.

He still had some beard to be made, but I didn't think that he was going to do anything about it anytime soon. He liked the little scruff on his face, I could tell. I could also tell that it had some gray hairs, which was puzzling. He looked a little older than me, but not by much more.

It certainly made him look sexier, I thought.

It was like time was frozen around me and all I could see were his eyes on me. It was almost as if they were burning through my soul and reading everything I was thinking. His eyes were icy blue, perfect as they were. They had a hint of warmth in them, but for the most part, they were freezing cold. So much so that I found it difficult to imagine that he could feel empathy for anyone.

I could see his Adam's apple bobbing up and down, showing me that he was a little nervous, even though he was hiding that fact well. One could look at him and think that I was going crazy about it, that someone like him could never feel nervousness, but that wasn't what I was seeing right now.

His body had such a presence that I didn't just feel small before him, but also incredibly warm, especially down there. My pussy was hotter and wetter than when I bumped against him. The last thing I thought could happen now was that I was going to stumble on someone so sexy and hot, whose harsh facial features were a sight to behold.

I noticed that he dropped the book that he was taking with him. I crouched, reaching out with my hand as I grabbed it. I slowly stood up as my eyes scanned his body from bottom to top, taking in the fact that his feet were enormous. For a brief moment, my mind recollected that saying that 'big feet meant having a big cock', but I quickly brushed it off.

It was just a joke and a silly one at that.

I lifted my hand that was holding the book. "Here. I'm so sorry I ended up bumping against you. It wasn't my intention," I said, trying to make it so my voice didn't sound too weak, even though doing that was almost impossible in the presence of such an imposing man.

"It was nothing. I know that it wasn't your intention. Not to mention that I should have paid better attention to where I was going, anyway."

When he spoke, I noticed that his accent was different, although I couldn't put my finger on where it came from. It was certainly from a European country, though.

And the door behind me opened just when I remembered that I came here for something else. *Sofia, that bitch.* She was going to pay for stealing my comb.

My eyes glared at her when I realized that she was looking at me with those same cynical eyes. She was with the elbow of her arm propped against the doorway, resting her head on her hand. She didn't have her shirt on, which was a sin in on itself. I couldn't even stand looking for more than a fraction of a second at her.

Seeing that, I turned my head quickly the other way, saying, "Just give me my comb back. It's what I came here for."

"Really?" She asked, her eyes immediately going up and down, I noticed even though I wasn't looking at her face anymore. She was checking out the man that was right behind me and whose name I didn't even bother to ask. My mind was such a whirl-wind of thoughts that that didn't even cross my mind. "Because I thought you were trying to hit on Leonardo."

Leonardo? I knew his name had to be different from what I was used to, but I didn't think that it was Italian. I slowly reopened my eyes, looking at his face and seeing something different. I was seeing the face of a man who was probably heading back to his home country. I supposed that the ship was heading to Italy, then.

Nevertheless, I had to brush that thought out of my mind right away. It served me no purpose.

I turned to the right slowly when I felt that something was in the corner of my vision. It was the comb that was so dear to me. Sofia was holding it in her hand, I noticed as I also took note of the fact that she was chewing gum. Gosh. Could she be any more dis-gusting? I asked myself, realizing that that question was pointless.

I reached out with my hand, grabbing the comb.

Leonardo grabbed the book from my hand, his hand cupping mine. It was at that moment that I realized that his hand was big and heavy. So much so that it made my hand feel smaller than normal.

He was so dominating, I could tell. I couldn't help but wonder what he was like in bed, not that I was thinking we had a chance of getting laid, though.

It wasn't going to happen and that was something I needed to keep in mind.

CHAPTER 2

"You are telling me you don't believe in love at all?" He asked, holding me close to his body. It was a strong, built-like-a-tank body. His eyes were on me as we kept ourselves afloat in the water. His legs swung gently under it, trying to teach me how to do it. I didn't know how to swim, which was something that deeply ashamed me. Well, now I was finally doing something about that.

"I don't," I replied, my eyes diverting downward and checking out his lips. They were rosy, perfect as they were. He had a slight overbite, which was excitably sexy. Just looking at his lips right now, I wanted to kiss him, even though I shouldn't.

And one of the reasons for that was that he was the one my father wanted to marry me with. And being with him, him being my swimming lessons teacher, wasn't something that I thought I would end up stumbling on while I was on the ship.

His body was perfect, with almost no body fat. I could feel his abs pressing against my belly, making me want to move my hand where they were and to slide it over their curves, feeling every ridge and crevice.

Given the look in his eyes, I could tell that he thought the same. He was naughty and I wasn't going to deny that.

Screams, laughs, chatters, and splashes of water around me told me that I wasn't alone, which was a good thing. I didn't know what would be happening right now if we weren't. If we were alone, I was pretty sure that he would take advantage of me, which wasn't something I wanted.

One of the things I didn't even want to think about right now was the fact that he was hard. I could feel his hard-on pressing against my pussy through my bikini. And it was big. His package was massive, bigger than anything I thought I knew. He was probably even bigger than most guys on porn movies.

"That's a shame. I was wondering if I could win your heart over," he teased, his lips dangerously close to touching against mine. I studied his eyes and I wondered if he was thinking the same thing. I didn't want to do it, but the fact was that I had never kissed anyone and here I had this beefcake almost kissing me. I was almost wondering if I shouldn't just do it. "I thought you were going to love me."

The aroma coming out of his mouth was minty. It went into my lungs, impregnating it with its smell. I could do nothing against it, and it was melting my body. Even though I struggled against his embrace, it was a weak attempt.

I chuckled. Gervasio could be quite the joker when he wanted to.

And yet, that was nothing more than just one thing that I quickly brushed off.

I wrapped my arms around his shoulders, pressing more tightly against his body. My boobs were pressing against his chest, and he loved that. The look in his eyes was telling of that. It wasn't lying to me about that.

He opened a big, bright smile, saying, "Wow there, I didn't think you were going to do that," and then he lowered his arms around my body, following the curves of it, eventually settling his hands on my asscheeks. He cupped both of them with them, making me emit a moan.

"Gosh, that's so good," I murmured into his ear, betraying the fact that I didn't want to fall in love with him. I shouldn't. He was going to do unspeakable things to me if I did.

Nevertheless, his body was just so warm right now and extremely inviting, and I could do nothing against that. Then, as if to tease me even more than he already was, he slipped one of his fingers under my bikini, locking his eyes with me one more time.

I had to admit it. It was difficult to read what he was thinking.

"Do you want me to go on?" He murmured into my ear, widening his smile. What a jerk. I knew that nobody was going to find out. We were in the swimming pool on the ship and the water covered part of our bodies, but Gervasio was still taking a huge risk. If anyone dived underwater, they could notice it. And if that happened, I would be so flustered I wouldn't know what to say.

"Yes…" I responded and it was the only thing I could say. My pussy was so wet and it wasn't just because of the water. My orgasmic juices were leaking out, and Gervasio was aware of that. So much so that I was pretty sure that, regardless of my answer, he would have gone on.

"That's the answer I expected from you and it's the right one, too," he continued. His finger moved left and right around my ass-cheeks and then he glided it toward my asshole. I wanted him to go further down where my pussy was, but he was always such a tease. Gervasio wasn't going to do everything I wanted.

Moments later, his finger was where he wanted it to be. On my asshole, prodding it. He knew how to brush his finger in all the right directions and when to use all the right speeds. My body started to shake, my eyes closing slightly.

Gervasio was turning me on in front of everyone while he still pretended that he was just teaching me how to swim.

He dipped his head, putting it close to mine. Everything was even warmer around me than it was moments ago.

"People are going to find out," I tried to warn, but the widening of his smile on his face told me that he didn't care. Gervasio was like that.

"And, what about it?" He hissed, his lips pecking my lips all of a sudden.

It happened so suddenly that I didn't know what to do. I just bulged my eyes out before shooting him the following question, "What the hell was that?"

He slipped his finger inside my asshole, making me moan. "Oh, baby. You know exactly why I am doing this. You think I'm a monster, that I kill people for sport, but that isn't the case. You hate me so much and yet you melt in my arms like this."

His dick was raging in his underwear, and I couldn't help but feel that I should do something about that. The only problem was that I didn't even know what to do. Even though we were having such a sexy moment together, I had no experience with what was happening.

And that lack of experience was showing right now.

"Maybe I should just kill you right now," I threatened, moving around with him in the water. His finger was still inside my rectum and I didn't think he was going to take it out of there anytime soon. Gervasio was tormenting me right now and he knew he was doing that.

"You won't. I'm going to make you come so hard right now that you are going to be questioning if you should continue hating me."

I bulged my eyes out one more time. I knew that what he just promised was the truth, or at least it was going to be so in a matter of seconds. I bit my bottom lip hard because I didn't want anyone around us to hear it. If they did, they wouldn't just kick me out of the swimming pool area, but also out of the ship.

I knew that my father was powerful and influential, but he wouldn't stand against them for me.

"Please, stop…" I begged him, but I didn't think he was going to listen to me. I was so right about that that he continued to rub and spin his finger inside my rectum, driving me crazy. "Everyone is going to hear us."

"Oh, let them hear everything. It's not like they can do anything about it, anyway."

I curled up the side of my lips, hating the fact that Gervasio barely even listened to what I murmured. What a jerk, and yet he was a jerk that I was beginning to fall in love with. Even though I hated him as a person, he was going to be the one to take my virginity. There was no denying that.

Moments later, when I started to hump against his junk and he bumped up the pace with which his finger was destroying my asshole, I finally came. My body started to rock and shake, and it was only thanks to the fact that his arms were keeping me locked with him that nobody around us noticed anything.

I could almost close my eyes and fall asleep, but I didn't. Gervasio was impeding me from doing that.

CHAPTER 3

Curled up in the bedsheets, all I could feel was the gentle sway of the ship as it continued to cruise the ocean. I was thinking back to what happened that afternoon when I was with Gervasio. His room was on the other side of the ship.

I… I was pretty sure that tonight he was going to come for me.

I was so sure about that that I kept the door open. It was unlocked and he could just open it. I had nothing more than my bra and my pair of panties on. If he found me in the condition that I was in, he would feel ashamed of me.

I twisted gently under the bedsheets when I started to hear footsteps coming in my direction. They were like gunshots sounding in the hallway, the person that owned them certain that he was coming where I was.

The room where I was on the bed was dark and everything around me was quiet. I twisted my body in the bedsheets one more time, my pussy hot and wet. Gervasio gave me that amazing orgasm while he was teaching me how to swim, but it wasn't enough. I wanted him to take my virginity. I wanted him to come inside of me.

All these years with my family keeping me locked up in my room, allowed only to venture outside some days so that I could walk around in the property, turned me into a slut. So much so that the only thing I could think about was sex.

I couldn't help but wonder just how big his slab of meat was, and it looked like I was going to find out the answer to that soon. A man just put his hand against the door, opening it. I heard it creaking, but it didn't bother me. Even though the ship was dead silent, nobody was going to pay any attention to what was happening in my room.

I curled up when I heard him closing the door. I was pretty sure that it was Gervasio. It had to be. He was the only one that knew I was in this room on the ship.

"Gervasio?" I asked, wondering if he was going to answer me. But when he didn't, I wasn't surprised. I knew he wasn't going to answer my question. So much so that when he sat down on the bed, I knew he wasn't going to say anything, which he didn't. "Please say something," I still pleaded.

He chuckled. My eyes were open, but I could only make out the silhouette of his body. He didn't have any clothes on. I could see the curves of his muscles under the dimmed light coming from the moon and through the small window of the room.

A moment later, he settled his hand on my leg, keeping it there for what felt like minutes. I wondered if he was going to do any-thing else, and I wasn't surprised when I felt his hand gliding up. He was looking for my ass, and maybe even for my cunt, and he was going to stop at nothing.

I tried to move my leg, but then he clasped his hand around it, stopping it.

"Why?" I asked, even though I knew he wasn't going to answer me. "Why are you such a jerk?"

Once again, Gervasio said nothing. He didn't have to. When he grabbed my leg, I knew that he said he didn't want me to move it. He wanted me paralyzed and frozen just like I was, as if I was a painting.

His hand was heavy and calloused. It was the first time that I was feeling a man's hand that was like that.

Gervasio knew who he was and the power that he commanded over me. In light of that, I wasn't surprised, not even in the slight-est, when his hand went to where my pussy was. He snuck one of his fingers under my pair of panties, touching my clit.

He started to rub it over and over as the seconds passed, and they were passing dangerously slowly. I moaned louder than ever before, not knowing for how much longer I could stand his wrath.

I just wanted to hear his voice one more time and I knew that he wasn't going to say anything, which was such a dangerous torment.

Then, he stopped making circular movements with his finger. When he wasn't rubbing it anymore, I felt that I could finally breathe again. And breathe I did, but only for a couple seconds. If I thought that just one of his fingers was enough to drive me crazy, I knew that a second one was going to be even more excruciating.

He leaned over, his body on top of me. I could better make out what the curves of his muscles were like, finally bringing enough strength to put my arms around his body. My fingers pressing against the hardness of his muscles, I just wanted him inside of me. His fingers were inside of me that time when we were swimming, but I craved something more.

"What are you doing? You're taking your time and that's pissing me off," I hissed, knowing that he wasn't going to take that well. And he didn't. He increased the speed with which his finger was rubbing my clit and then stopped what he was doing.

He started to play with my pussy folds, gently sliding his fingers against them. As he continued to do that, I roamed my hands around his body, making sure that I wasn't hurting him with my nails.

He huffed slightly and then kissed my shoulder, making his way upward. I parted my lips moments before he kissed me. We started to make out and his tongue immediately went inside my mouth. We then shared a short tongue battle, and it was so brief that I didn't even realize it was over when it already was.

His fingers lingered against mine when he grabbed my hand. His hand was so big that mine felt incredibly tiny, and I knew that any ounce of resistance I still had against him just crumbled.

When he pulled his head back slightly, a line of drool still connected our lips.

And in the meantime, I slid my hand downward, finding his ass. For a moment, I thought that his asscheeks were slightly different from what I was used to, but I didn't give that thought much importance. I was just happy that I could bathe in the warmth of his body, feeling the softness of his asscheeks.

And then, I did something I thought I wasn't going to. I snuck my hand under his pair of boxer briefs, which was the only piece of clothing he wore. I thought that he wore nothing when he stepped inside the room.

I moved it around his waist before finding what I was seeking. It was his hard, raging cock. The moment I felt it, I flinched, but only for a fraction of a second.

Even though I couldn't make out his face in the darkness, I knew that he just smiled.

Then, he lowered his head as he planted his lips against my neck. I arched my back, and then I responded to that by wrapping my fingers around his cock. It was so big that my hand felt tiny again, which was something I realized was a constant between us.

Gervasio still played with my pussy folds and it appeared that he wasn't going to stop doing that anytime soon. As the seconds ticked by, I realized that I was on the verge of orgasming again.

"You are such a jerk and I'm going to keep saying that until you finally say something back," I muttered, each word hurting me.

Just like all the other times, as if he was doing everything in his power to hide something, he kept his lips sealed.

I started to pump his shaft over and over, and it didn't get any harder than it already was. He was ready to penetrate me, to breach me with his man tool, and I couldn't wait for that any longer.

Then, he retreated his hand and grabbed my hand – the one that was grabbing his cock. He made me pull it back, which I did even though I didn't want to.

For a fraction of a second, I wondered what was going to ensue, and then I realized what his endgame was. I widened my eyes at that same moment. It surprised me. It more than did that, in fact. It shocked me and I could do nothing about it.

"What are you going to do now?" I asked the same moment that he tore off my pair of panties without warning. One moment it was protecting my pussy against him and the next it was nowhere to be seen.

    And when he spoke, I just realized that he wasn't Gervasio.

CHAPTER 4

In fact, he was someone else entirely. He was the same man whose name I didn't even ask when I bumped into him when we were in the hallway. If my eyes were already wide before, now they were as if they were going to jump out of my head.

I lunged away from him, but then he just grabbed my legs all of a sudden. His grip was strong and determined. Even through the darkness in the room, his eyes glared at me.

"You aren't going anywhere, little princess," he said and his voice was the same that I had heard at that time. I should be trying to kick him, but I couldn't. His grip was just so strong that I couldn't even move my legs an inch.

"You are hurting me," I said, noticing that I just lost that rising feeling of an orgasm that was going to wash over me. If this man was thinking that the way he just popped up in my room was going to make me fall in love with him too, then he had something coming.

"What's your name? So that I can report you to the police."

He straightened his back slowly, regarding me with his eyes. For a moment, I thought he wasn't going to say anything, but then he replied, "It's Leonardo. You should already know that about me. Do you have dementia or something like that?"

I slapped at his shoulder, feeling furious at what he just insinuated. "Of course not. I'm just angry at what you did. I was expecting someone else."

Sofia did tell me his name before. I must've forgotten it for a brief moment.

I could still feel the pressure where his fingers were. It was like they were still there. The way he just showed up in my room unannounced would forever remain in my mind and, at the start, it was a huge turnoff, but now I couldn't stop thinking about it. And in return, my pussy was beginning to get hotter, too.

"Who were you expecting? That loser that wants to be your husband?" He growled, making me wonder if they had some kind of history between them that I wasn't aware of. Nevertheless, I made no questions about that. I didn't want to involve myself with something I didn't have anything to do with, at least not on the surface.

And after a moment of silence, he asked, "Did you like what I was doing?"

I bit my bottom lip. I didn't want to admit to this asshole that he was right about that, but I also felt offended by the way he just showed up in my room.

When he noticed my reaction, he said, "I'm really sorry about the way I just showed up here. It won't happen again, I promise."

I studied his face for a couple of seconds, trying to find out if he was telling the truth or not. When I realized that that was nothing more than a fruitless endeavor, I just shook my head.

"I'm not going to say anything," I said, my voice low and throaty. I wasn't going to admit to this jerk that he was right about anything.

In light of that, I crossed my arms over my chest, pouting.

He leaned over slightly, being so close to me that I could feel his minty breath. It was intoxicating and it was also making it very hard for me not to keep looking at him.

"I like it when girls like you make it harder for me. There's nothing like beating a challenge."

"Fuck you!"

"No," he said, widening his smirk, "I'm going to fuck you."

The moment he said that, I expected that he was going to lunge at me, but he didn't. He stayed where he was, his eyes confident and staring at me.

It was like he was reeling me in with his stare alone. Fighting against his wrath was pointless. He wanted me and I craved him. Gervasio made me feel so good, but he wasn't here and, as time passed, I began to think that he wasn't going to show up.

"He isn't here. I'm going to do so much more to you than what he can," Leonardo promised, grabbing my legs again, but this time he was much more gentle. It was like his hands were made of silk. Whatever strength I had before just melted and there was nothing I could do about that.

"Can you promise me one more thing?" I asked, my voice sounding like I just begged.

Hearing that, he slid his hands further up until they were almost touching my pussy. I thought he was going to do it, that he was going to begin tormenting my cunt with his fingers again, but it was obvious that he had other plans in mind.

"Whatever you wish, my princess," he purred, kissing my right leg once and then twice in a row. His lips were just so warm and wet, which was exactly the way I wanted them to be.

"Can you do it slowly?"

For a moment, the question hung in the air and I had no idea if he was even going to answer it. When I was already growing nervous and frustrated at his lack of response, he replied, "Of course. I'm going to do it much better than Gervasio did. It will be slow and, sometimes, even painful, but things will be better. I'm going to do it so much better than he did that you will think at least five times before getting married to him."

Hearing that gave me the relief that I needed. I then closed my eyes, tilted my head backward, and widened the gap between my legs.

Leonardo broadened his smile, kissing my legs again, and this time the kiss was much slower than the first one – and also the second one. It was as if his lips melted my skin. The longer that they were in contact with it, the stronger I felt that I was going to pass out.

My breathing quickened, sweat started to come out of my pores, and I gripped the bed sheets tightly. He was relentless, making his way up as he kissed me from the lower part of my legs to where my cunt was.

But then, Leonardo stopped. I thought that he was going to quickly resume what he was doing, but then I realized that he froze up. I opened my eyes again as I realized that he was still smiling.

"What? Thinking that I was just going to stop like this and leave you hating me?" He murmured, moving so that his head was right between my legs and no more than a couple of inches from my pussy.

He thrust his tongue out, flicking it over my clit. Each flick sent shockwaves of pleasure through my whole body, making it shake and rock. I gripped the bedsheets so tightly I thought I was going to tear them. My vision started to blacken and I even thought I was going to pass out for sure this time, but I didn't.

I was still right where I was, on the bed, my lungs begging for air.

"That was delicious, wasn't it?" He asked, lowering his hands so that he was cupping the region just under my ass cheeks. "And there's much more from where that came."

I didn't even try to question him about that. I knew that he was certain about what he just prophesized.

He then lifted my legs and shoved them over his shoulders. My pussy was lined up to his dick and I just noticed that a bead of pre-cum was coming out through the little slit.

For a moment, nothing happened. Leonardo was just taking in what his eyes were seeing.

Even though it was dark, his eyes behaved like they were from a cat. He could see all the curves, the wetness coming from my womb, and the way my pussy folds pulsed.

"God, you are so perfect..." He murmured, sliding his dick right inside my pussy, and he met no resistance other than my hymen. When the head of his cock was pressing against it, he thrust his hips forward slightly, popping it. It happened in a fraction of a second. I didn't even have time to notice what was happening before it was too late.

"Should I go all the way in? They want me to do that?" He murmured into my ear, nibbling on my earlobe.

I didn't even know if that was a real question or not. I just nodded. It was basically the only thing that could be done.

Then, seconds later, he started to roll his hips slowly. His pace was excruciatingly slow in the beginning, taking his time. What he promised before was coming to fruition. He was doing this so slowly I knew it was going to take me a lot of time until I hit my orgasm.

CHAPTER 5

And it happened. That same night, he took my virginity, and… then never showed up again. I was still on the ship, fighting against the motion sickness that came with it. I looked through the whole structure for Leonardo, but couldn't find him. I had no idea where he went or what his intentions were, but it was obvious that he wanted me just for that one-night stand and that was it.

I was so pissed off that, when I received a letter weeks after that, I wanted to tear it. I wanted to tear it until it was nothing more than hundreds of pieces.

I was gripping the letter so hard my knuckles were going white. I flipped the letter in my hands again and again, hoping that I was going to catch the name of the person who was playing this joke on me. I mean, we didn't dock anywhere, didn't stop for anything at any port, and we had phones and everything we needed to keep in contact with the people we loved.

It was for that reason that I didn't even want to open the letter, even though I was tempted to do so. I sat on the bed, barely aware of my dress. It was a tight fit. It fit nicely around my body, highlighting my curves. I knew that because Sofia said that I looked good. Considering that she hated me, that compliment meant a lot.

My fingers were shaking, but it was okay. I then pried open the letter slowly, fishing out of it a small piece of paper. It was ripped. The sides were ripped, as if someone did whatever was behind this hastily.

"Whoever is playing this joke on me is going to pay for it," I muttered, shooting up when I realized that I recognized that handwriting. I thought he wasn't going to come. I thought he wasn't on the ship, but now he wanted to meet up with me? This whole time, avoiding me even though I always went everywhere on the ship, always trying to make new friends and get to know new people?

I had no idea what was going on in his mind, but I had to make a decision.

I was pondering what decision I was going to make when I remembered that soon we were going to be docking at our final destination. Once we were there, I wouldn't be able to continue living in this dream.

Leonardo took my virginity, made me feel impossibly good, and I wanted more of that. I had no idea if he somehow fell off the ship, but even if that happened, I could have whatever I wanted with another man.

Gervasio also started to avoid me. I wondered what was up with that.

I crumpled the piece of paper and the cover of the letter with my right hand, tossing the ball into the trash bin. Standing up, I started to make my way toward where the piece of paper said I should meet up with Girolamo. He said he was going to be there, and I had a million questions to ask him. None of them were going to be easy, but they had to be made anyway.

I crossed several hallways, rooms, and whatever else the ship had until I got to the other end of it. I was in a place where I could see the ocean and some blocks of ice floating on it. It was cold, but not too much. Not to mention that I was still inside the ship. It was just that, from where I was, I could see everything thanks to the glass panels that replaced what were supposed to be walls.

I put my hands on my waist as I turned my head left and right, pouting. I was already getting furious at the fact that he wasn't here. Girolamo said that he was going to be here, and he was never someone that didn't do good on his promises.

While I was in my high heels, I murmured, "Where the fuck

are you?"

Moments later, when I thought that he really wasn't going to show up and that this was nothing more than a ruse, I turned around as I felt a hand settling on my shoulder.

I flinched for a moment. The last thing I thought was going to happen was someone putting a hand on my shoulder.

Fisting my hand, I was ready to punch his face until he was begging for mercy when I realized that he was none other than Girolamo himself. It had been such a long time since the last time I met him, and I was shocked at how much he changed over the years.

He looked exuberant, handsome, and excessively sexy.

He had a dark suit on with a red tie, making him look even hotter than he was. He was my college crush, from the time when I thought I knew about everything in the world. His beard was made, looked sharp, and his hair cut short and licked to the side.

His eyes were dark green, regarding me with impossible curiosity. He was much taller than me, and it was as if he grew even taller than when we were 19. His presence was unmatched. Not even the guys that I met on the ship were like him in that regard.

He retreated his hand slowly, letting his arm fall to the side of his body.

"Miriam, you came. I thought you weren't going to. I know about everything that happened while you were on the ship. I just showed up here, but I've been following you. They want to kill you."

I took a step backward, not knowing if I should feel more lust for him or if I should be scared of him. What he just said was out of this world. People wanted to murder me? Who?

I didn't know if I believed him, but the determination in his eyes showed me that he wasn't kidding when he said that.

"What do you mean?" I asked, stepping farther away from him because it was the only thing I could do right now. It wasn't just his appearance that was different, but also the way with which he carried himself. It was almost as if he was an assassin.

"It means that I came here for you, and there's no time to

explain why," he said, marching toward me and cornering me against a wall. I felt my butt bumping against it and I realized that I could go no further.

He planted both of his hands against the wall behind me. Then, lowering his head, I didn't try to stop him when his lips touched mine. An electrical shock traversed my body, making me feel waves of pleasure and lust.

When I said I wanted to continue making my dream a reality on the ship, I didn't think that things were going to happen so quickly and suddenly. His lips were soft, sweet, and also incredibly wet, which was just the way I liked them.

It was as if our kiss went on for hours, even though it couldn't have been more than seconds, I thought when he retreated his head, blinking once and slowly.

I could only wonder what was going on in his head right now.

"What the hell was that?" I asked, noticing that he wasn't moving away. If anything, he was standing right where he was, his eyes gazing into mine.

"I'm going to save you, that's what's going to happen. I'm going to take you away from here."

"But how?" I asked when he kissed me again, his lips rubbing vigorously against mine, wetting them and turning me into stone, or almost. I couldn't move my body, melting in what he was doing to me.

I had difficulty breathing. I thought I was going to die suffocated, but then he pulled away without warning. When I reopened my eyes, I noticed that he was already taking off the coat of his suit. He tossed it to the side and then his hands went to where the buttons of his shirt were. As he undid one of them after the other, I knew what was going to happen and I wanted every second of it.

He was going to have sex with me as well. I didn't think it possible, that three hot men were going to fuck me while I was on the ship.

His eyes went up and down, taking in what they were seeing.

"And given that they can't know where you are right now, I'm going to fuck you. It's what I've always been thinking about ever since we graduated from college."

"What?" I squeaked, but it wasn't like he was even thinking about answering that. One moment he was standing where he was and then, the next, he was butt-naked. I knew he worked out, and that his body was built like a tank, but I didn't think that he was so good-looking.

We didn't have the same age gap that I had with the other guys, but it wasn't like the age difference mattered so much right now.

All I knew was that his cock was big and that I wanted to be all over it.

When he noticed the wicked smile on my face, he said, "I knew you were going to change your mind about it so soon."

"I'm beginning to think that you aren't so different from those other guys..."

I went to my knees right away, taking in what my eyes were seeing. It was his shaft, standing probably in front of me, making me drool and lick my lips.

I lifted my hand slowly, carefully wrapping my fingers around the circumference of his shaft. It was hot, blood pulsing in his veins. I tugged at the skin slowly and then wrapped my lips around his mushroom-like cockhead, loving the feel of it against them.

It was a mouthful. His cockhead was just so big that it stretched my lips beyond any level I thought possible. I swirled my tongue around it, and then one more time, and then one other time, until I felt like I couldn't have enough of it.

His balls were unattended and I couldn't let that be. Realizing that, I cupped them with my hand, playing with his balls. Even though things just barely started, I knew that he was already on the verge of having his climax. So much so that I started to slow things down. I didn't want this to end so quickly.

His balls were heavy and laden with his milk. I knew that because they were also lovingly warm. So warm that it was impossible for me not to be playing with them for what felt like hours. In the meantime, I kept bobbing up and down on his cock, feeling every inch of it. Well, not every inch of it because I didn't want to start to gag.

I wasn't going to deep-throat this man. If I did that, it would be like committing suicide.

He put his hand on my head, dictating the pace he wanted. I just kept on doing what I was doing, tasting his pre-come. As the seconds passed and I realized that our fun was ending, I decided to speed up things.

Moments later, he exploded inside my mouth. Rope after rope of his come, he shot his milk inside of it, allowing me to taste its salty flavor. It was intoxicating and almost like a drug. I couldn't have enough of it and I was pretty sure that I was going to be dependent on it.

When I pulled my head back even though I didn't want to, I noticed that my lips were coated with his come. What he was seeing made him smile.

And then, after putting his clothes on, he grabbed my arm and announced, "Come on. We're leaving now."

CHAPTER 6

I could do nothing to stop him as he put me in the helicopter and then we took off toward the coast. It was relatively close. So much so that I was able to see it from the helicopter the moment that we were hovering over the ship. For the next few minutes, I was already on the coast, in a hotel, and forgotten about. I was forgotten by Girolamo and I didn't even know where he went.

I knew that it was a mistake what he did. He shouldn't have left me alone. What if the other guys came here for me? They had their chance to kill me when we were alone and squandered it. I was pretty sure that they were coming for me.

It was for that reason that I looked outside the window of the tiny apartment where I was. It was dark outside, the moon high in the sky and the clouds around it. Everything was quiet around me and I could even hear the slow beatings of my heart.

I sighed, turning around slowly when I realized that I could finally hear something weird. For a moment, I thought that it was coming from down below, from the street, but then I realized that it was actually coming from the sky.

I just looked up and noticed that it was a helicopter, piloted by a man. It took me a while to notice it, but I soon figured out that the pilot was none other than Gervasio himself! The man that was supposed to become my husband was coming for me, and the glare in his eyes told me that he didn't like that I'd fled.

I flustered, pacing around the room and cooking up a plan. I had to leave the room somehow if I wanted to avoid them coming in here and getting to me. If that happened, I didn't know what would then ensue. They'd surely kill me. Even though I thought several times a day that living wasn't worth it, the last thing I wanted right now was to die.

I was just thinking that I was going to leap into the elevator and then out of here when the door slammed open. I let out a little scream, noticing that one of the men that did that was none other than Leonardo himself.

He had a gun with him that was tucked in his waist and it had a silencer. I didn't want to think about what he was going to do with it. He was probably going to kill me.

I was in the kitchen and so my hand snatched a knife. I held it in front of me while pointing it at them. Leonardo held up his hands, but the wicked smile on his face told me that he wasn't afraid of me.

"What do you think you're doing now, princess?" He asked, stepping toward me and then wrapping his fingers around my wrist. I didn't try cutting him with the knife. The power that he held over me was nothing short of incredible, and I knew that I was supposed to do everything he wanted.

"You came here to finish the job," I accused, lowering my eyes.

He planted his hand on my chin, lifting it. "Who said that? Frankly, I'm disappointed that you just up and left in that helicopter. Who did that with you?"

"I'm not going to answer that. I don't want to put his life at risk..." I responded.

"You already are by not telling us the truth," he said, squeezing my wrist slightly so that I dropped the knife. A short, brief clink echoed in the room and then he took me to the kitchen island, where he made me sit on it.

He lowered his head, moving it around my neck and shoulders.

He sniffed me, closing his eyes slowly while Gervasio stepped toward us and then started to play with my breast.

"We are actually fighting for you. When this is over, you'll have to tell us what you really think about us, who you prefer," he murmured, finally making something in my mind click.

This was why this was all happening. They were fighting for my love, which was something that flattered me.

Suddenly, I also realized that if they really wanted to kill me now, they'd already have done so.

And so, I had no choice but to fall into their embrace of me, my nightie suddenly being pulled up, and there was nothing that I could do about that. Gervasio was then all over my boob, mauling on it and loving my nipple with his tongue. When I looked down, he even met my eyes, telling me a million things through them.

Then, his hand found my thigh, going up and encountering my little snatch. He skipped my clit and went straight for the honey pot, slipping a finger inside of it. He moaned and then murmured something that I couldn't make out, even though I was pretty sure that it had something to do with the fact that he was in love with me. Or just with my boobs. Regardless, it was hot and it was making it difficult for me to breathe.

Leonardo, in the meantime, wasted no time before finding himself between my legs. He put both of his hands on them, moving them aside slowly. He widened the gap between my legs and then lowered his head. When he put his tongue outside his mouth, I knew what he was going to do and I braced myself for it.

Gervasio crashed his lips against mine, putting his tongue inside my mouth moments later. We had a short tongue battle, and it didn't last much more than a couple seconds. It made sense that it didn't. I was nothing more than a little princess for him and I needed to keep that in mind.

Nevertheless, when he took hold of the kiss, I thought I was going to pass out. A moment later, I felt my body lying on the kitchen island, with both of the men standing on top of me. One was pleasing my cunt however he could and the other was doing unspeakable things to my pair of boobs.

"I don't know how you managed to stay virgin for so long until I took it," one of the guys said and I didn't even know who it was. All I knew was that one of these men was lapping up at my snatch, making my whole body shiver. In the meantime, the other was roaming his hands over my breasts, kneading and fumbling with them.

I thought I was going to climax and I wasn't surprised when it happened. All I knew was that my body started to shake violently over and over. I thought I was going to pass out and the only thing keeping me from doing that was the fact that I could feel both of these men on top of me.

"Wait!" I begged them, reopening my eyes before I noticed that a shadow was standing behind them. For a moment, I thought that it was a stranger, but then I realized that it was just Girolamo. The glare in his eyes was telling. He didn't like an ounce of what was happening and wanted revenge.

I thought about sitting up and begging him not to do anything, but then I realized that he was curling up the side of his lips. I thought that that was weird, but then it lasted only a couple of seconds.

"Well, boys. I knew you were hungry for her, but I didn't think that you were *this* hungry."

He wasn't against them. Girolamo was actually with them, with Leonardo and Gervasio and I thought that such a thing was impossible.

He waved his hands and they both went to the side, making space for him. A second later, he was the one between my legs. He grabbed my thighs and started to knead the skin with his hands. They moved excruciatingly slowly, feeling the smoothness and softness of it.

"I went out for only a couple of minutes and you are already in deep trouble with them," he murmured, lowering his body as I figured out what he was going to do.

With his tongue out, he started to lap up at my pussy, making me arch my back. My cunt was so wet I knew it was never going to be like that again in my life. Girolamo was relentless, sometimes licking at it quickly, other times slowing things down.

When he realized that I was already far too exhausted to continue, he grabbed me, turned me around gently on the kitchen island, pulled me down slightly until my feet were touching the floor, and then slid his dick right inside my cunt. I felt it going all the way until he was touching the end of my tunnel.

"I'm a little disappointed. I still have some inches left," he murmured, rolling his hips soon after. I started to moan and groan, matching him thrust for thrust. I was wild and realized that he was just the first man. The other guys were going to pound in and out of me as well, and it was going to be jaw-dropping.

He picked up his pace and I soon started to come, my body rocking back and forth over the kitchen island. I bit my bottom lip so hard I drew blood out, and that wasn't even the tip of the iceberg of my climax. I was panting, more exhausted than I was before, and feeling so dirty. And it wasn't just that, too. I felt more than dirty. I felt filthy.

Moments later, he pulled out. He did that so slowly I thought I was going to fight back to keep him inside of me for as long as possible, but I didn't. The reason behind that was also a very simple one. I looked up and then to the sides, seeing that the other guys were already coming where I was. One of them grabbed my thighs, pulled me toward him gently, and then eased his prick inside my womb.

I could feel his hands all over my body as he started to rock his hips forward and backward. Differently from Girolamo, he was relentless from the get-go, his balls slapping against my ass. Slapping sounds started to fill the room, blocking out everything that was happening around me.

And then, he came inside of me, filling me with rope after rope of his viscous sperm. It was warm, thick, and creamy. When he pulled out, a line of milk lingered between the slit of his mushroom cockhead and the entrance of my pussy, and it was so hot.

It split moments later, announcing that it was time for the last guy to have me. And he did that. He was already all the way inside of me even though he still had some inches left. I was disappointed that I couldn't have all of them inside of me, but I wasn't going to moan about that much.

All I knew was that I was already hitting another orgasm when he came inside of me too. They all did and, if they knocked me up, I wouldn't know who the father was, and that was… Okay. I wanted to be with all of them.

That was my final decision and nobody was going to change it.

LOVING HER AGE GAP

CHAPTER 1

My pants and a pair of panties stretched over my ass as I bent my body down, elongating my calves. I was trying to reach the tip of my toes, but I couldn't. A couple more inches and I would be able to, but not this time. My calves were already in pain, and I was trying to get one more inch further down, stumbling on the same counter-resistance from before. My body just didn't have the elasticity.

The conversations, the laughs, and the silly jokes around me reminded me that I was still in the gym. Outside, it was hot, the sun making everything bright. I could hear some cars driving on the road in front of the gym, but it was nothing more than background noise to me.

The gym was packed with men and they were mostly young, or several years older than me. When I said 'several years older than me', I meant guys already in their mid-thirties. Even as I did my exercises, I couldn't help but steal glances at them. They were still so hot and sexy I couldn't help but imagine what they were like when fucking someone like me.

I stood up slowly and straightened up my back, brushing my forearm along my forehead. I felt beads of sweat clinging to the skin of my forearm. Remembering how much I hated feeling that I was sweaty, I turned to the left and opened my backpack. It was small, but serviceable. After moving the zipper all the way to the right, I fished from inside the backpack what I was looking for. A single, yellow flannel, not too light and not too heavy, and perfect for me to keep myself dry.

I straightened up my back again and then swiped the flannel on my forehead, drying it.

For a moment, I thought that eyes were on me, but then after lifting my eyelids, I didn't find anything unusual. I thought that I was going to spot one of the guys glancing at me, but I didn't see anyone. All I could see was guys pumping weights and running on the treadmills.

I had just gotten to the gym. I was still trying to stretch and loosen up my muscles, and I hadn't even started my exercises properly. Thinking that, I put the flannel on top of one of the machines in the gym and then bent my body down again, hoping to reach my feet.

I strained myself as much as I could, really pushing for that goal, but I made no progress. I could feel sweat pooling on my forehead again when, suddenly, I felt a hand settling on my shoulder, pushing it.

It was a heavy, strong hand that could belong only to one of the older men at the gym. For a moment, I froze up. I thought that it was forbidden, at the gym, men touching women the way he was doing and without my permission. And in the meantime, my mind was already going back to something else.

I was a virgin. Even though I was already 19, I was saving myself up for the right man, and the reason behind that was pretty simple. I was a hopeless romantic and I was always going to be so. It was just the way I was.

Sometimes, though, I was over-the-top naughty and couldn't care about romance. Trying to figure out what was going on in my mind was complex and tiresome.

The way his hand was pushing down on my skin, finally making me reach my toes was exotic and alluring. He wasn't using much weight, nudging my torso down just enough so that my fingers could touch my toes.

For a moment, I considered peeking over my shoulder, but I didn't want to spook him. I was just happy, even though momentarily, that my fingers were touching my toes. I finally achieved something as a gym amateur, and I was just so happy that I could almost not contain myself.

I could feel his fingers through my skin-tight shirt, loving how dominant and heavy they were. The only thing that was weird about this was that he hadn't said anything yet. Nevertheless, I was sure that he was going to, whoever this man was. He was probably just one of the personal trainers.

A few seconds after my fingers scraped over my toes, he retreated his hand, letting it fall to the side of his body. I stood up slowly as I turned around at the same pace. My eyes went up and down as I then took in what I was seeing in front of me. I was right when I thought he was one of the guys in his mid-30s, but I didn't think he was so lust-inducing, and especially that he was one of my crushes at the gym.

He had a dimmed smile on his face, some scruff that covered the lower part of it, dark green eyes, and a nose that was just the right shape and size for the form of his face. I could see chicken feet on the sides of his eyes, and they grew more evident when he widened his smile slightly. His hair was licked backward, looking sharp and wet, though the latter was most likely because he was just as sweaty as I was.

He wore a white, flimsy gym shirt to cover some of his muscles, but it wasn't enough. His arms weren't covered and my eyes could feast on the perfection of their lines. Even though he wasn't flexing his arms, I could see where the shadows started and stopped and how his muscles just appeared to be wanting to rip out through his skin.

I couldn't help but wonder what I would feel if I were to fall into his arms. He would hold me safe, take me tightly, and I would spread my legs open for him like the slut I was.

One thing my eyes suddenly caught on was the fact that his body was covered with tattoos. They were painted in black and some of them were names. I didn't know who those names belonged to, but I wasn't going to ask him about that right now. And one of the reasons for that was that the moment just wasn't right.

Most of the time, I was confident, but being in the presence of such a burly man was making me feel like I was much younger and unsure about the kind of person I was.

My eyes diverted down when I noticed something that I should have overlooked. It was his hard, enraged dick, poking against his shorts. I blinked twice, wondering if I was dreaming this, but when I realized that nothing changed, I knew that things were about to get sizzling hot.

"Hi, I'm Mike," he said and I paid attention to the way his lips moved. His teeth were perfect. They shone under the light of the sun coming through the glass panels that composed a portion of the walls. And his voice… It melted my heart. "I just saw that you were having a hard time stretching your calves and I thought I should come and help you."

I brushed my fingers through my hair, shaking it to the side. I then opened a big, uncomfortable smile before replying, "You were a great help. I don't think I would've been able to do it without you."

He stepped closer to me, so close that I could smell his sweat, or maybe that was just the natural scent of his body. Regardless, it was intoxicating and it filled my lungs. For a brief moment, I almost couldn't breathe.

"Do you come here often? I could help you again," he proposed, locking his eyes with me as I just noticed what his intentions were. I felt heat rising to my cheeks as I didn't know how to act right now. Given how inexperienced I was, I was having a hard time even choosing my next words. "And I have all the time in the world for that."

I felt my nipples going hard, the thought that I might finally lose my virginity sprouting in my mind. His presence was a little unnerving, but very much welcomed.

"I'm just starting out here. I don't know if I'll be coming here often."

"Maybe I could change your mind about that…" He suggested, putting his arm around my waist and then taking me away from there and toward where the bathrooms were.

I was a little flustered, but I was still going along with his plans for me. His arm was heavy and confident in the way he was holding me. One step after the other, we went there, and I knew that things were going to shoot up to the next level in about a couple of minutes.

Or maybe in even less time than that.

CHAPTER 2

The bathroom was for women only, but he didn't stop before opening the door and then locking it with a key. I didn't even know that he had the key, but he wasn't ashamed when he used it. He turned around slowly, flipping up the light switch to bring life to the light bulbs. Everything was suddenly bright around me and I could make out the perfection that his body was once again.

"This should give us a little more privacy..." He teased, stepping toward me after shoving the key back into his pocket. "And you haven't even told me your name yet."

"That's something I should rectify," I said, trying to sound more serious and composed than I was. The truth was that my heart was beating with the speed of a machine that couldn't be controlled anymore.

"Oh, I like the sound of that."

Mike finished stepping toward me, putting both of his hands on my shoulders as he pressed me against the wall. His fingers were digging into my skin as he lowered his head, making me think that he was going to kiss me. I thought I was going to lose the virginity of my mouth right then and there, but it didn't happen. It didn't because, right at the last moment, when our lips were a fraction of a second from touching, he pulled his head back.

He wiggled his finger in front of me as he leered. "It's not going to be so easy, princess."

What a tease he was. I knew that the first guy who was going to have his eyes set on me was going to torment me with all the foreplay that he could muster, but I didn't think that it was going to be like this. So much so that I was already feeling disappointed, even though my nipples were telling a different story. They were rock-hard, poking against my shirt and bra.

Seeing that, he didn't stop before moving his hands up and pinching both of my areolas. He twisted them slightly, eliciting a moan out of my mouth. I shut my eyes then and there, moving so that my body was pressed against his.

As he continued pinching both of my nipples, he lowered his head before landing his lips on the side of my neck. They were scalding hot and wet, and they stayed in contact with my neck's skin for what felt like forever. He sucked on it, leaving a hickey. When he pulled his head back again, he smiled devilishly.

He was always such a tease and now was no different.

"Are you going to take my virginity?" I asked, pouting. I knew that I looked like a slut, but I didn't care. What I cared about was him giving me the right answer. "I need that so much."

He scraped his fingers over my lips, replying, "I might just do that."

His words melted my heart again and I fell into his arms, loving the way that he was holding me so tightly without hurting me. I could feel his muscles against my skin and how beefy he was. I thought I was strong, but he was showing me how wrong I was. He was the dominant one, the alpha man at the gym, and that was putting it mildly.

He snuck his fingers under my shirt, lifting it up and over my head. He then tossed it to the other side of the bathroom, which was big enough for a large crowd to take showers in it. It was a communal bathroom, after all.

"I love how smooth your skin is. Younger women are always especially delicious," he cooed into my mouth, making me think that our lips were going to touch and that he was going to kiss me for the first time, but that didn't happen. He just breathed into my mouth, eliciting a moan of pleasure out of it. "And I love how submissive you are."

"How could it be any different?"

"The answer is that that is just impossible," he replied, taking me away from the wall and then against the other wall that was on the other side of the bathroom. He was gentle when he threw me against it, but also firm. Mike was the kind of guy who always wanted to assert his dominance and now was no different.

He ravaged me with his eyes and they shot up and down, taking in what they were seeing. They stopped where my boobs were and then he took a deep breath.

"I knew they were big, but seeing them in person is something else," he breathed through his mouth, dipping his head slowly before grabbing my right breast with his hand. He then wrapped his lips around my nipple, sucking on my areola for what felt like minutes, but were certainly only seconds.

When he retreated his head, my nipple was soaking wet and hot. It was so hot I thought my skin would never go back to normal. I just reopened my eyes and then I figured that this really might be the instance where I was going to lose my virginity.

He took half a step closer to me, pressing his body against mine. The warmth coming out of him was all around me, destroying any resistance I still had against him.

I had to do something and so my hand reached down for his cock. I grabbed it through his pair of shorts, encircling my fingers around it. Feeling that, he shut his eyes slowly and then let out a moan of pleasure.

"Gosh, that's so good."

Mike kissed me on the crook of my neck again, paving his way down until his lips were wrapped around my other nipple – the one that he hadn't sucked on yet. His eyes shot up before he said, "I'm going to do you so good right now you'll never be able to forgive me."

"Please. That's what I want. Give me everything I want and then some more."

He curled up the side of his lips again and then thrust down my flimsy pair of shorts, falling to his knees so that his head was right in front of my pussy. He shot his tongue out and started to lick at it, each lick slow and powerful, making ripples of pleasure surge in my body. They hit every part of me, making me think that I was going to come right at this moment.

He gave it another long, reverberating lick and I thought I couldn't take any more. I felt heat rising inside my body, like a tidal wave and then crashing when my orgasm hit me like a train. My body started to convulse and then my vision began to darken. I thought I was going to pass out, but then his hands gripped my waist and legs, reminding me that I was still here. I wasn't in the safety of my house where I could do anything and everything without being found out.

I just couldn't let that happen. If my father found out that I was having sex with a stranger, he would destroy my life.

After another long, everlasting lick, Mike stood up slowly while gliding his hands over my body. They halted at my shoulders and then moved until they were on my neck. Mike grabbed my neck, but his fingers weren't digging in.

"Suck me off…" He commanded and I could only obey. I fell to my knees right then and there, easing my fingers under his shorts before pulling them down until they were at his knees.

His dick sprung out proud and threatening, big and thick. I licked my lips then and there, encircling my fingers around it. My hand was tiny in comparison and that only served to turn me on more than I already was.

"And don't take long. I don't have that much time," he warned and I knew I had to hurry up. Thinking that, I started to stroke his shaft slowly and carefully, loving the fact that his pre-come was already seeping out.

When I felt that I was already better used to his size and length, I shut my eyes and then took the plunge, closing my lips around his mighty cock. I started to work on it immediately, doing everything I could so that he got closer to his climax. He started to moan and then put his hand on my head, dictating the pace that he wanted.

Pre-come still leaking out of his little slit, I loved its salty taste, savoring as much of it as I could. I swirled my tongue around his mushroom-shaped cockhead and continued to bob up and down along his length, though I was careful not to put too much of his shaft inside my mouth. I didn't want to take the risk and start to gag.

Then, his shaft erupted inside my mouth, feeding it with his come. I swallowed everything and he pulled out with an exuberant smile on his face.

After we got dressed again, he opened the door and gave me his phone number, but not before two other men showed up when we were stepping outside the bathroom.

The glare in their eyes was telling. They knew what happened and wanted to ask us severe questions about it.

CHAPTER 3

I thought I was doomed then and there, but that wasn't what happened. They were just his friends. Their names were Rigo and Tancre and after a little talk, they invited me to their yacht. It was massive, cruising just outside the beach area. It was dark outside, the moon high in the sky and the stars twinkling around it.

The environment around me was serene, other than the laughs, the chatters, and the pounding music behind me, that was. People stumbled over as they tried walking from one spot to the other on the yacht and I could even hear the occasional sound of glass shattering on the floor of the ship when a drunkard's glass slipped out of his hand.

We were having a party and it was enthusiastic, messy, and welcoming. I was supposed to be a part of it, but I wasn't. I was sitting by the swimming pool with my feet in the water. My legs swung shily in the water, my mind elsewhere.

I was thinking back to Mike and when I thought he was going to claim my virginity. He promised me he was going to do it, but then he didn't.

I was with my bikini on, a glass of wine by my side. I thought about drinking it, but I didn't want to. I wanted my head to be clear because I had no idea what was going to happen aboard the yacht.

Glass shattered behind me again, making me snap my head backward. I spotted a large, hairy man lifting his hand as he clenched it. In front of him was another guy about his size that was also raising his fisted hand. The glare in their eyes was unmistakable. If no one stepped in, they were going to have a fight, and that wasn't something that I wanted to witness.

As if someone was reading my mind, hands appeared out of nowhere between them, pushing both men to both sides. They tried to punch him, but he dodged their attempts without breaking a sweat.

When he was between them and then he lowered his arms, he said, "No fighting on the ship. I'm not going to tolerate that, and that's not why we are here, anyway. We are here to have fun."

Wow, I whispered to myself, finding it hard to believe that Rigo was able to do that so effortlessly. When he realized that those men weren't going to give him any more trouble, he stepped away from them. I looked behind him to see if they were going to re-initiate their fight, but they didn't. They grumbled something I couldn't make out and then stepped away from that part of the ship.

Rigo came toward me and then stopped. He held out his hand before saying, "Want a little help getting up?" He asked, his voice just like I remembered it. I was thinking that because since that time we first met at the gym, I didn't speak to him until now.

I grabbed his hand and then he pulled me up. I lost my footing for a moment and then I fell into his arms. He opened a devilish smile as he laughed at what I had just done. I was almost behaving like I had drunk too much, even though that wasn't the case.

"Woah there, Zohar. You shouldn't be so careless like that," he advised, taking me away from the pool and I didn't do anything to stop him. "You could hurt yourself doing things like that."

He then lowered his arm so that it was around my waist and he took me back inside the yacht. We were in a hallway where nobody else was. Everything around us was quiet and all I could hear was the pounding music coming from the outside, but it sounded so distant it was almost like it was coming all the way from the beach.

I glanced up, remembering that I was with someone else who had a huge crush on me.

His eyes went up and down, studying me, examining every

curve of mine.

"Mike did what he did that afternoon and I'm still bitter about that. He shouldn't have felt that he was allowed to do that."

"What?" I squeaked, but I knew that my half question wasn't going to be answered. The moment he said that, he put his fingers under my bikini and then tore it off like it was nothing. I knew that he was strong, that he had rippling muscles, but I didn't think he was capable of doing something like that.

Seconds later, the bikini was on the floor and I was utterly exposed. Noticing what was happening, I jumped into my horny and slutty mood. I wrapped my arms around his neck and let my body fall into his arms.

"Do you like what you see?" I cooed, crooning against his neck. I started to hump my body against his, needing to feel my pussy against his dong. It was hard and raging and I could feel it through his shorts. He didn't have a shirt on, which was perfect. It meant that I was going to have an easy time savoring his body for everything that it was.

He had blonde, cut-short hair, and the front was combed up. His eyes were bright blue, shining into my soul. His face shared harsh lines, his jaws taught and square-y. And his lips... they weren't too thick or big, they looked so succulent. I couldn't stop looking at them and thinking how much I wanted to kiss them.

"I do," he replied, his voice suddenly throatier than normal.

When I remembered that we were still in the same hallway, I asked, "Shouldn't we go somewhere more private?"

"Why?" He widened his devilish smile, grazing his fingers against my clit. He started to brush them at it slowly before picking up his pace when he felt that he was close to making me orgasm. I was so desperate to climax that I knew it wasn't going to take long until that happened. "I don't think we should. After all, this is my ship as well."

"You surprise me by saying that, *captain*," I said, grinding my body against his for what felt like an eternity. I couldn't help but wonder what his shaft was like when it wasn't under his shorts. They were so flimsy and thin and I knew I could pull them down easily. I just needed his okay, or maybe not even that. Point was, I was going to have his dick one way or another. "I never thought you were brave enough to go up against your buddies."

"You don't know what I'm capable of," he growled, shoving down his shorts without giving me a warning. He didn't need to, after all. When they were down and his dick sprung out, I already knew what I needed to do. I jumped and threw my legs around his waist, rubbing my snatch against his humongous rod.

I thought he was going to love it, that he was going to want me to do that, but then his eyes grew gloomy.

Lolling my head back and forth and with a dumb smile on my face, I asked, "Something wrong? Am I doing something you don't like?"

My hand was still brushing against his shaft when he responded, "Nothing. Just that I remembered something."

Without warning, he pushed me gently off him, making me put my feet back on the floor. I raised one of my eyebrows as I cocked my head, wondering what the hell was going on in his mind.

When he snapped his eyes back toward me, I knew that whatever had just passed through his mind didn't matter anymore. He threw his arms around me and picked me up, walking with me in them toward somewhere. Where that was, I had no idea, but I knew he was going to do unspeakable things to me.

"I thought you were going to take my virginity?" I asked impishly and he looked down at me with threatening eyes.

"Do you think I should? Is that what you want?" He asked and I nodded. Mike could be such an asshole sometimes, I noticed.

He chuckled and then took me to the other part of the ship, which was on the other side from where most of the party was happening.

Out here, nobody was going to find out what he had in store for me.

CHAPTER 4

He laid me down on the lounge bed, spreading my legs. Rigo was then between them, bending his body until his head was right in front of my waiting pussy. My body shivered and I was afraid of what he might do, but I was still willing to go all the way with this.

Rigo didn't straight out say that he was going to claim my V-card, but I was pretty sure that that was one of his plans.

He sniffed my cunt, closing his eyes slowly. When he reopened them, he was staring right into my eyes. "I love the smell of a soaping cunt," he murmured, making my body shiver again. I felt shivers all over my body, my skin like that of a chicken.

"This is so unfair," I grumbled, breathing the air around me. It was sea air but, this time, it felt different. I felt like I was truly alive. The prospect that I was going to finally lose my virginity was eating me up from the inside out.

"Why?" He asked, settling his hands on my thighs and then moving them up and down slowly. *Dangerously* slowly, I corrected myself. The way he was doing that was almost enough to make me come then and there. I thought I was going to, but then I pushed it back. I didn't want to do that.

"You are taking your time and I hate foreplay," I said, writhing and feeling like time was suddenly infinite. The longer this was taking, the more I felt that I would never become like my friends, who weren't virgins anymore.

He raised his hand, his finger brushing against my clit. "You need to be patient. I'm going to do it. I'm going to take you in ways you can't even imagine and I'm going to make you so happy you'll wonder how you stayed a virgin this whole time."

"You fucking jerk," I hissed, my hips bucking before he pressed his finger to my clit and then circled it slowly. Not satisfied with that, he lowered his hand, playing with my pussy folds, massaging them.

He pulled them to both sides, opening the gap where my tunnel was. Rigo's eyes studied it for a couple of seconds and then he dug inside of it with one of his fingers, spinning it in there for what felt like hours.

I shut my eyes one more time, my whole body resonating when I thought that I was going to come then and there. But that stopped when he pinched my clit slightly with his fingers. I shot my eyes open again. I couldn't believe that he just pushed back my orgasm like that. If there was something that I just couldn't stand, it was orgasm denial.

"You shouldn't do that and I don't forgive you for committing that sin."

Seconds ticked by, his eyes holding me intensely, and he said nothing. Rigo was excellent at pissing me off.

"You aren't going to let me come?" I asked, my tone impish and lacking vigor. I shouldn't even have asked that. The smile that crept up on his face was telling.

"Not yet," he said, dipping his head one more time before sticking his tongue out. It was no more than a couple of inches from my cunt, ready to claim me as his woman. "And, I like playing with my food, too."

"I should slap you so hard that teeth would come out of your mouth after saying that," I hissed, moaning once more when he swirled his tongue over my pussy folds, tasting my come.

"And yet, you aren't."

"You're making me regret my choice. I don't think I need to tell you how much I hate that when it happens."

"You're going to feel whatever I want you to feel right now," he hissed into my pussy, his dick still out and pointing at me. I glanced at his mushroom-like dickhead, loving it, wishing that my lips were worshiping it and not doing what I was at the moment, which was nothing. I was letting Rigo torment me with his tongue and fingers, and I couldn't do anything about that.

He circled his hands around my thighs, kneading my skin. Not satisfied with that, he lowered them until they were under my ass-cheeks. Rigo started to knead my skin and do everything else that he felt entitled to. He even dug in with one of his fingers before he started to prod my asshole. I arched my back in response, signaling that he could go on.

I widened the gap of my ass slightly and he traced his finger over my orifice, feeling every ridge and crevice. "Oh gosh, this is almost too much," I murmured, smiling briefly before moving so that I could kiss the crook of his neck. Then, I nibbled on his earlobe gently.

"I knew you were going to say that," he said, his fingers still moving over my orifice, pressing against it. When he was used to what he was doing, he decided to take things a step further. He eased one of his fingers inside my rectum, drawing circles with it inside of me.

Each time that his finger completed a circle, my toes curled and I thought I was going to climax again. I felt waves of heat surging in my body. I never thought that he was going to be so cruel, that he was going to take so long to steal my virginity.

"You are a monster for what you're doing to me," I said, moving my hips up and down so that I could feel his finger better. It was a gigantic finger that seemed to fill my butthole easily. I couldn't help but imagine what his shaft would feel like inside of me. Probably too big and painful, I guessed.

"This isn't even the beginning. There're so many crazy things I want to do with you."

"Just pop my cherry already."

He smiled without showing his teeth, leaning over so that his lips were almost touching mine.

"Maybe not right now," he joked, taking his finger outside of my rectum, which was something that made me feel like punching him again. And I was going to do just that when I realized that his hand was already back on my thigh again, sliding up and down over it, feeling my skin and kneading it. "But I still love you for the person you are."

"Fuck you."

"Heh. I think I'm going to be the one doing the fucking right now," he joked, turning me around and then helping me with lifting my butt. I parted my ass cheeks a little wider than before, inviting him to come in. I couldn't peek over my shoulder, but I was still certain that he was already planning on impaling me with his shaft.

My pussy was soaked and pulsing-hot, and also more than ready for this.

He dipped his head and then slithered his tongue out of his mouth, giving my pussy a long and everlasting lick. My body trembled. I almost lost it then and there. Breathing was just so arduous now, especially when I had such a dominant man behind me, licking my cunt over and over.

"You are so tasty," he said, moving so that he was closer to me, positioning himself behind me. He was on top of me, his body creating a shadow that blocked some of the light around me. I could feel his slow, controlled breathing against the side of my neck and his dick grazing my ass. Rigo was going to do it, wasn't he? He was going to fuck me. Rigo was going to be the first to take my virginity and run away with it.

"I promise not to scream much."

"We'll see about that," he said, rolling his hips as he started to rub his shaft against my ass. The movement was controlled, even slow, but he knew what he was doing. I could feel his long, massive shaft moving up and down between the crack of my ass, almost like he was jerking himself off with it.

A moment later, his lips were by the side of my right ear when he asked, "Do you like what I'm doing? Do you want more of it?"

"I want everything," was the only possible answer I could give him, and that I did.

He gave the side of my neck a peck and then dropped to his knees, still positioned behind me. I braced myself for his forceful entry. I knew it was going to be painful and memorable, but then… I started to hear friction sounds, which puzzled me.

He was jerking off and was going to come all over me! The first thought that popped up in my mind was how disappointed I was. I thought that Rigo was going to take the virginity of my asshole, but it turned out that that wasn't his plan.

Seconds later, he moaned loudly before he started to spray his milk all over me, aiming for my ass. I felt it covering it, and it was white and thick. It was also incredibly warm, making me realize how wrong I was when I thought I was disappointed.

When he was done, he moved away from me and pulled his shorts back up. I scooped up everything I could with my hands and then started to lick my fingers clean, enjoying the salty taste of his explosion. As I licked one finger after the other, he looked at me with disdain.

"I didn't think you were so slutty. I mean, I figured you might be, but I'm still impressed."

"I want you inside of me. Why didn't you do it?" I asked, my voice so feeble right now. Noticing that my finger still had a gob of his sperm, I licked it off too. I didn't want to miss anything. I wanted all of his milk inside of me and I was making that happen.

I blinked once and slowly as I waited for his answer.

"You're going to learn the truth soon."

And with that said, he turned around slowly and started to walk away. I was left dumbfounded and with a million questions in my mind.

Why did Rigo refrain from taking my virginity when he could?

CHAPTER 5

I was lying on my bed, bored, texting on my phone when I realized that streaks of light were just sneaking through the window of my room. The sun was coming up, which meant that it was already morning. I didn't sleep at all during the night. During the whole night, I kept thinking back to when I almost lost my V-card. I thought that they were going to do it, that at least one of the guys was going to claim me for himself, but then Rigo and Mike stepped away like they finished their duty.

I was so bored I slid my legs off the bed, dropped my feet on the floor, and with nothing more than a nightie on, I started to walk down the corridor outside my bedroom. I then reached the outside of the ship and stopped to take in what my eyes were seeing.

What a mess. I took a step forward, pulling my foot back so that I avoided stepping on shards of glass on the floor. I reached down with my hand, finding a used condom. Well, at least someone had sex while I was feeling frustrated with Rigo. Craning my head to the right, I spotted more shards of glass. It was almost like someone had a fight here. The boomboxes were tumbled over, I noticed, which was a pity. It almost looked like they were broken. That particular model, from that brand, was expensive and worth millions.

I stood up, beelined to the left when I noticed pieces of paper all over the floor, lines of cocaine on top of one of the bars, and small pieces of crumpled paper still with marijuana in them. My eyes also spotted some used cigars and cigarettes, though I didn't think much of them. It was obvious, from the start, that the people that came for the party were also going to be smoking a lot in it.

And it was fun. I had a lot of fun with them.

I was just turning around when I felt a hand on my shoulder. For a moment, I flinched, thinking that it was someone seeking to do something terrible against me, but then I calmed down when I realized that he was none other than Tancre.

He was only with his shorts on, making me wonder what was behind them. I was pretty sure that he was as hung as his friends. His hair was of a shade of coconut, cut short, and he didn't have a beard on his face. His cheeks were slightly rounder than those of his buddies, and he looked a little younger, but the tattoos on his chest spoke a different tone. His skin was slightly tanned and I could see the outline where his sunglasses were.

When he opened his mouth to form a smile, I noticed how white and perfect his teeth were. He probably frequented the dentist often.

When he pulled his hand back, he said, "Did something happen? You look spooked."

"I'm just in shock at seeing the state in which the place is. I didn't think that the party was going to leave such a mess for you, and I want to say that I didn't have any involvement with what happened. I behaved when they were thrashing the place."

He waved his hand, dismissing my concern.

"It's nothing, really. This is why I have employees who work diligently for me. They'll clean up everything." And without warning, he looped his arm around my waist, taking me away from there. We strolled through the interior of the ship and stopped when we were on the other side, by the swimming pool where I almost lost my V-card. I was still so disappointed that it didn't happen. Though, now that I was thinking about it, it might happen with Tancre.

His arm was still around my waist as if he was thinking I was his possession. I just might be, I thought with a hint of humor in my mind.

"What is it that you do for a living? Other than working as a personal trainer…" I had no idea if I was crossing a line that he didn't want to be crossed, but I still had to do this.

He turned around slowly, being so close to me that I could smell the perfume that he sprayed on his body. It had a woody hint in it and it wasn't as strong as I thought it was. It was there, noticeable, but there was just a slight hint in the air of it and not much more than that. It was totally different from the floral perfume that I sprayed on my body before the party started last night. This morning, so bored while I was in the bed, I didn't even bother doing that.

"Do you really want to know what I do for a living?" He asked, moving his arm so that it was over the upper portion of my back, his muscles straining against it. It wasn't that he was exerting himself right now, but that his muscles bulged and flexed easily without him even thinking about that.

"Yeah, I'm kinda curious about that," I replied, my heart speeding up when I noticed that his head was lowering and he was about to kiss me. I had already sucked off a shaft and it was amazing, but I still hadn't kissed. Was he finally going to be the one who was first going to do that for me? I didn't know, but the thought was in my mind and I couldn't brush it away.

"Do you really want to know?" He asked, putting his hand under my nightie and then moving it up, finding my breast. I didn't have a bra on. I thought I was going to just lie on my bed and fall asleep, but that didn't happen, obviously. It was just a waste of time, in the end.

I nodded once and slowly, keeping my eyes locked with his even though doing that was difficult. His lips were so close to mine I was pretty sure he was going to kiss me, and yet he didn't. At least, not initially and not while he was just staring at me without speaking.

"I kill people. I rob them. I do things you don't even think possible, and I make people's lives a living hell. That's what I do for a living."

The way he said those things, I could think that he was just joking, but I knew that it wasn't the case. He said those words so coldly I knew that they expressed the truth.

His hand started to knead my breast, his fingers pressing against it and pinching my nipple over and over. I melted, my knees wobbling. His other arm went around me, holding me in place.

When he widened his smirk, I knew that he loved my reaction.

"Wow there, Zohar. No need to act like that when things just started."

And I was going to say something back to him when, all of a sudden, his lips crashed against mine, finally kissing me. All the air that was in my lungs gushed out against his face. He sniffed it, taking it all in, and the glint in his eyes told me that he loved the smell.

"You should do that more often," he murmured against my mouth, brushing his lips against it. Not satisfied with what he had just done, he dug his tongue into my mouth, battling against my tongue. We had a short battle, and it was extremely brief. In no time at all, it was over and he was in full control of the kiss.

Finally, after the disappointments I had with Rigo and Tancre, someone was going to take all of my virginities, my pussy included.

CHAPTER 6

His tongue was still inside my mouth when I realized that we weren't alone. I thought that everyone on the ship was still sleeping, but then I heard footsteps approaching us. They were footsteps from two huge guys, I could tell. The way they sounded so heavy and loud told me as much.

I tried peeking over Tancre's shoulder, but I couldn't. His shoulder kept getting in the way of what my eyes could see. But then, I had a glimpse of what was happening. It was, just like I thought, Mike and Rigo, and they didn't look pleased with what their eyes were witnessing.

When Tancre finally noticed that I was busy with something else, he looked at me with questioning eyes, raising one of his eyebrows. "Something wrong, love?" He asked, moving his hands down and cupping my asscheeks. He was still grinding his body against mine, rubbing his junk up and down against my pussy, willing me to open wide for him. But I couldn't do that. Not when it seemed that things were about to take a turn for the worse.

Their stares were threatening. They were thinking about hurting their buddy in ways I couldn't even think possible.

"We all want her and we thought that we had an agreement," Mike hissed, shooting toward Tancre, latching his hand on his shoulder, and yanking him away from me with all the strength he had. His colleague fell heavily on the floor and then jumped back up, standing on his feet in a fraction of a second. The look of danger in his eyes exuded out of them and I was pretty sure that he was thinking about picking a fight with his buddies, though I had no idea if he was willing to go all the way.

He assumed a fighting stance, fisting his hands in front of him.

"You think that I'm willing to share?" He growled, looking at me for a moment before returning his glare to his buddies. "I don't do that, especially when it's obvious that you were just fucking with her and not doing the right thing. Zohar, tell them how disappointed you feel right now."

"Uhh, what?" I squeaked, not really understanding anymore what was going on right now. What was that thing that they were saying about sharing me? I couldn't wrap my head around it.

"Tell them!" He shouted all of a sudden and I could do nothing more than to tell the truth.

I nodded once and calmly, replying, "I thought that you were going to make me happy, but you only left me disappointed."

Mike then said after softening up his face. "Well, looks like we have a duty to finish then."

Tancre parted his lips and let his arms fall to the sides of his body, straightening up his back and looking more relaxed now.

"You mean that we're finally going to do it?" He asked and they all approached me, surrounding me. I felt tiny and unprotected, just like my pussy and asshole did. They eyed me up and down, analyzing me like I was nothing more than a rat that was being studied. "We're finally going to pop her cherry?"

The mention of that fluttered my heart, making me realize that all the time I spent on this ship was going to be worth it. They weren't just going to pop my cherry, but also claim me in ways I never thought possible.

Rigo glanced at his buddies, replying, "I think it just might be the time for that." He regarded me with lustful eyes and then asked, "Are you ready for that, Zohar?"

I cleared my throat, suddenly feeling that it was incredibly dry. For a moment, I didn't even know what to say. All I knew was that I was frustrated before, thinking that these guys were only thinking about playing with me as if I was a toy.

My pussy was burning hot right now. I knew what they looked like when they were naked. They were perfect, like gods.

Not thinking twice about it, I grabbed the underside of my nightie and pulled it up and over my head, exposing my bare body for the delight of their eyes. They dissected me with their pupils, the glint of lust in them more than obvious.

Then, they pulled down their shorts and underwear, showing me their dicks again. They were massive, raging, and pulsing with their veins. They looked so mean that I was already feeling threatened. I didn't even know what to do, my lack of experience showing.

"Are you afraid of what might happen?" Mike asked, stepping toward me and then taking me to the swimming pool. My right foot tried finding the floor again, but all it did find was the air and the water under it. I looked at his eyes, wondering what he was thinking, and then I realized what it was. I threw my mouth open at that moment, thinking that he was out of his mind, and then he fell down with me into the water.

I felt my body surrounded by the water and being immersed in it. It wasn't cold or warm. It was lukewarm, which was perfect. I tried to swing my legs quickly so that I didn't drown, remembering that I didn't know how to swim, and at the same moment realizing that a pair of arms were holding me with my head just above the surface.

And in front of me was Mike. He had a smirk on his face, as if he knew he was in control of me and could do anything he wanted to me.

We were swimming butt-naked in the swimming pool, which wasn't something I didn't think I was going to do while I was on the ship.

"Did you think I was going to let you drown?" He asked, gliding his hand down my body and finding the crack of my ass. He brushed his finger through it, eliciting a moan out of my mouth. I had no idea why I was so easy to be pleased, but it was happening again and I was doing nothing about it.

"I thought that you were just fucking with me."

He widened his smirk. "I'm going to do a lot more than that."

And having said that, he lunged away from me, and I panicked.

I thought I was going to drown. My arms flayed around in the water and I tried to swing my legs in a more controlled manner, but it didn't work. I was sinking into the water, my nose already inside of it when a pair of hands pulled me up so that my head was above the level of the water again.

What a jerk. I thought he was going to keep holding me safe in his arms. I didn't think he was going to disappoint me the same way he just did again.

I reopened my eyes as I found out that it was Tancre who was in front of me and was holding me up with his confident arms.

"We have a nice, little surprise for you," he murmured into my mouth before crashing his lips against me again, kissing me. We started to make out and I soon forgot about what Mike did. His lips were wet, especially thanks to all the water that was around us. They were also lovely warm, exciting, and welcoming. We started to smooch with our tongues and our kiss was certainly much more passionate. I didn't think that it was possible to stop it even if I wanted to.

"What surprise are you talking about?" I asked even though it was difficult to move my lips when he was still kissing me with everything he had. He smiled gently for a brief moment, moving his hands so that they were cupping my ass cheeks, his fingers digging into my skin. He brushed them over it, moving them through the crack of my ass. I felt them brushing against my orifice and I thought he was going to pop my asshole's cherry, but I knew that his intentions were different from that.

In the meantime, I just realized that someone different was behind me. His hands went where my ass was and he parted my asscheeks, making way for his tongue, which started to lick my orifice even though we were still swimming in the water. One lick after the other, he showered me with pleasure, making me realize that it was possible to feel wanted by more than one man.

"This is unbelievable," I crooned, scratching my nails over Tancre's back, drawing blood out. I thought he was going to complain about that, but he kept his lips sealed.

What he didn't say, he expressed with what he was doing to

me. It wasn't enough that he was worshiping my buttcheeks with his hands – he started to slide his hands over my backside and then around my shoulders. One of his hands even latched around my neck, applying pressure on it and making me shoot my eyes open.

I thought that he was going to kill me or do something worse.

But then he eased his grip on it, moving his hand until it cupped my right boob. He played with it using his fingers for a little while, pinching my nipple over and over. I was pretty sure that, if I were lactating right now, I'd be shooting milk even while we were still inside the water.

And in no moment at all, I found something lapping up at my pussy. It was a tongue. It was hot and wet, flicking up and down, brushing against my sensitive skin. Each lick was powerful enough to send shockwaves of pleasure through my body, making me curl my toes.

I was beyond myself, leaking my cunt juices for what felt like minutes already, even though it couldn't be more than seconds since I fell into the water. They were loving me in all the ways they could, pleasing every sensitive part of my skin.

"God, you make me so hard," Tancre murmured into my mouth, tracing his way down as he kissed the side of my neck and then my breasts, fumbling with them as he used his fingers expertly.

I widened the gap of my legs when I felt Ringo moving closer, both of his hands on my thighs. He kneaded my skin while we were still in the water, his hands then playing with my pussy folds.

"I can't take this anymore. Just come inside of me. Just impale me already with your mighty shafts and make me your bitch."

I felt one of the guys propelling himself upward behind me, settling his hands on my shoulders before he murmured into my ear, "I think that the last part has already happened."

"Stop teasing me and just do what you need to do."

"As you wish," Mike murmured, putting his arms around me so that his body ground against mine and then he slipped his shaft inside of me, going in all the way. He was the one that was going to first take my virginity, which wasn't something I thought was going to happen. I thought that they were planning on doing that with a blindfold on my eyes so that I didn't find out who did it first, but it appeared that they were just doing things without prior planning.

With a long, strong thrust of his hips, he pierced my hymen and then went all the way where my cervix was. He pushed past it as well and bottomed out, letting out a moan through his lips when that happened. He was lodged inside of me and wasn't going to come out anytime soon.

I pursed my lips hard and shut my eyes. The waves of pain traveling in my body were beyond anything I thought possible. He was so deep inside of me that I could feel his balls pressed against my ass, and I loved that.

"How are you feeling right now?" He asked before pecking my neck for a brief moment, his hand roaming around my shoulder. In the meantime, his buddies were loving my asshole and breasts, doing everything they wanted with them.

"Like I'm on the moon," I replied and he wasted no time before he started to roll his hips slowly and carefully. Each time that I felt his balls pressing against my ass, I felt closer to reaching my orgasm. I moaned and groaned loudly each time that happened, just wishing that this was going to take all the time in the world.

But if there was one thing that I had already learned about life, it was that when things were good, they tended to end quickly. Mike picked up his pace, pounding in and out of me, ramming with his shaft without mercy, and then he came. He erupted inside of me without using protection and I knew that meant I was going to be knocked up.

And that thought, instead of panicking me, made me feel more lust than I thought possible. My flaming orgasm was burning so hot that it was already out of my control. I couldn't contain it any longer and so I came as well, my cunt juices flowing freely over his cock.

A moment later, he pecked the side of my neck gently and pulled out. When he was swimming away from me, Rigo replaced him. I had just about enough time to process what was happening behind me before it was too late. He thrust his shaft deep inside of me and bottomed out.

Unlike his buddy, he didn't ask how I was feeling, just rolling his hips forward and backward without mercy from the get-go. As I felt his ballsack slapping against my ass, I came twice in a row, my pussy juices flowing freely around his stick.

He pumped his sperm inside of me too and then slowly pulled out with a pop. I was panting and tired and if it wasn't for the last guy that was still holding me up, I would be sinking in the water.

When I thought that things were already ending, he swam around me, positioning himself behind me before he bent my body down. He repositioned himself and then thrust his hips forward, sliding his dick all the way and bottoming out, too. He started to fuck me with everything he had and then he came inside of me, making me wonder who was going to be the father of our baby.

I had no idea who that might end up being and, right now, it didn't matter. My eyes were tired and the guys were pulling me out of the swimming pool. I didn't fight back because I knew they were going to take me somewhere safe.

I just wondered what my life from now on was going to be like. Could I marry all of them? I didn't know, but I was hopeful I could…

The End

Looking for more Steamy Reverse Harem? Then, check this one out:

Sharing her Innocence

You can also read a sneak peek on the next page. Lastly, leave your review. I love reading your feedback!

TEASER: SHARING HER INNOCENCE

Series: So Big It Hurts - 1

Darlina was what her name implied, a darling. She was so innocent. Her bedroom's walls were still painted in soft pink, she had some plush toys she liked to have around and she played with her dolls sometimes.

She was an adult woman capable of making decisions for herself, though. Today was her birthday. She just turned 20 and was ready to face college again. She told me classes there were tough, but I just comforted her by saying that was how they were meant to be. College was never an easy thing to tackle.

Darlina was sitting below the canopy of a large tree in front of our home, back resting on the trunk. The book she was reading was about a princess running away from three scary peasants trying to sell her to another kingdom.

What a coincidence. That was just the kind of thing I was thinking of doing to her with some of my friends.

We had a very strong and unbreakable bond. Darlina and I lived together for a very long time. We could as well be more than what we were, but written and unwritten rules prohibited me from touching her.

She was forbidden, but so irresistible.

Her birthday party was over, though. She brought some of her friends. They were all nice people, but she wondered what my gift for her would be. "Don't worry about that. I have just the thing a woman your age needs."

Her being the innocent young one she was, what I was concocting didn't even cross her mind. She would never know until we were all over her.

But first, I needed to cross many lines. Just the thought of doing that was making my cock swell under my briefs. Had to control myself right now, though. Didn't want to make her think something dirty was going on.

I was in my bedroom, watching her through the curtain of the opened window. The sun was high in the sky and shadows were sharp. The day was perfect for the kind of thing that would happen.

Ending her innocence would be just as good as taking her virginity. How I wished Troy and Brock would hurry up. It wouldn't be long until she would lock her bedroom and not come out until it was time for dinner.

But then, maybe we could just force our way in.

Just admiring her now was enough, though, in a way. Her legs had smooth skin that shined under the light of the sun. Her cheeks were slightly redder than the rest of her body. Her nose was perfect and fitted her face like gloves on a hand.

Her hair was incredible. I couldn't stop looking at it. It was as if the quality of it didn't age one day ever since she was born.

Despite her innocence, she had features any man drooled over for. Those breasts were huge like melons. If she were to get pregnant, they would be even bigger and full of milk. I could just imagine myself drinking from them while rubbing her clit over and over.

Would she moan my name while asking for more? I could only hope so...

MORE BOOKS LIKE THIS ONE

SERIES - ONE WOMAN MANY MEN

This series is all about punishing backdoors, and these men have no mercy for their prize.

1. Filling Her Rear One
2. Filling Her Rear Two
3. Losing Control
4. Looting the Backdoor

SERIES - IN PUBLIC

This series features tough, dominating bossholes gangbanging women in public, and it's utterly shameless.

1. Fed from Behind One
2. Fed from Behind Two
3. Fed from Behind Three
4. Fed from Behind Four
5. Tight Squeeze

ABOUT THE AUTHOR

Leandra Camilli's obsession? Writing dirty, steamy stories that make her readers drool. She loves her Alpha males, hucows, sissies, and futas. If you're looking for those kinds of books, look no further.

With a cup of coffee on her table and warm socks on, she writes almost every day. Leandra Camilli has featured in several top 100 categories in the store, and she publishes weekly.